NEVER SAY DIE

He walked on. Sometimes he came to old snow-fields not yet eaten up by the Chinook and gathered handfuls of snow to chew on as he walked. Sometimes he came to small arroyos with water running in them. On through the moonlight he explored the folds and pockets of his rags, and found scraps of jerked meat that he sucked on. Sometimes he would carry the link in two hands and study it thoughtfully, then lay it on the ground and drag it behind him. And so he went on, slowly using up his strength, gradually putting more distance between himself and the banshee cañon. With his feet wrapped up until they looked like big bundles of hide, and, with the link leaving a furrow in the dust, his meandering track resembled that of some huge lizard dragging its tail.

He grew weaker and weaker. In the end, he rested more than he walked, lying for hours in the dirt and finally rousing himself to go on. Inevitably there was no strength left in him. . . .

RIDE TO BANSHEE CAÑON

James C. Work

LEISURE BOOKS NEW YORK CITY

LEISURE BOOKS ®

February 2004

Published by special arrangement with Golden West Literary Agency.

Dorchester Publishing Co., Inc.
200 Madison Avenue
New York, NY 10016

ISBN 0-8439-5319-5

Printed in the United States of America.

RIDE TO BANSHEE CAÑON

Preface

Of the legends recorded in Bulfinch's *Age of Chivalry*, none is more intense than the story of the knight they called Owain. Leaving King Arthur's court to find the Fountain of Life, Owain became the Guardian of that fountain and of the lady who lived there. But Arthur and Gawain came searching for him and brought him back to Camelot. After three years, the Lady of the Fountain sent her handmaiden to accuse Owain of unfaithfulness and betrayal.

Shamed by her public accusation, the knight fled to the wilderness. There he wrestled with his personal demons until he was reduced to living like an animal. Kindly people finally found him, starving and covered only in rags and animal skins, his hair long and shaggy. They nursed him back to life.

Under their care, Owain recovered his sense of self-worth. Then, learning that the handmaiden of the Lady of the Fountain was in peril, he set out to save her. And to say more would reveal the outcome of this novel, for it is true both to the Arthurian myth and to what I believe to be the truth of human nature.

Ride to Banshee Cañon is not based on any single historical event or set of characters, but I have drawn upon first-hand accounts in writing it. One valuable source was *Pulling Leather*, the 1884–1889 recollections of a cowboy, Reuben B. Mullins, who was also an expert blacksmith. W. P. Ricketts in his 1942 autobiography, *50 Years in the Saddle*, writes about Wyoming blizzards. After one blizzard, he and other cowboys discovered cattle that had frozen to death standing up. They also discovered two unfortunate trappers whose tent had collapsed in the blizzard and who had tried to walk to a homesteader's shack a mile and a half away. The cowboys found the frozen bodies; the trappers had only made it two hundred yards.

The fierce winds and howling blizzards of Wyoming are amply documented. But what I also found in Ricketts and in such books as Theodore Roosevelt's *Ranch life and the Hunting Trail* (1888) were descriptions of humor and loneliness, of frustration and perseverance. Anywhere you look in history, from the earliest chronicles to the most recent accounts, you can find stories of men going into the wilderness to confront raw, naked life, and discovering the limits of their convictions and inner strength.

For bits of real life humor and daily life on the frontier prairie I'm indebted to *Happy as a Big Sunflower*, the diary written by Rolf Johnson during the years 1876–1880.

I need to thank the good people of Chugwater and Douglas, of Casper and Saratoga for letting me poke around and ask questions about the big ranches of the old days. Thanks, too, to all the people responsible for the small museums in such places as Douglas, Encampment, Fort Robinson, Fort Laramie, Julesburg, Kearney, Strasburg, and Chadron. From their displays and collections I learned things about old quirts and bits of iron that are not in the history books.

J.C.W.

Chapter One

TAMING THE RANGE

The herd, range-fed and hand-selected, walked along peacefully, allowing the cowhands to drive them westward across the sweep of uplift where the high plains approach the northern Rockies. After the soft rains of May and June the grass was tender, the sage a lush olive color. The yellow and lavender smudges against the shades of green were clumps of wallflowers and tall locoweed.

In the shallow cañons and gentle draws, cottonwood trees lazily turned their leaves above the stiff branches of wild plum and scrub oak. A few birds called from the deep shade, but, otherwise, all was quiet except for the steady plodding pad of the cattle's hoofs and the occasional sneeze of a rider or horse. But in the space of a moment, as the cattle trudged closer to a swale holding a particularly dense tangle of trees, peace gave way to chaos.

The range bull exploded out of the thicket and headed straight for the herd, slashing his long horns from side to side. Steers and cows on the flank nearest him began to snort and roll their eyes, stalling with widespread front legs as they watched him come. Riding point, Link heard the sudden outburst of bawling, and turned. That tangle-tail longhorn spelled trouble, but, before doing anything about the bull, he had to calm down the cattle on the flank and make sure they kept walking. If every man stuck to his position and did his job, they would prevent a runaway. Farther back, Kyle was coming at a half gallop alongside the herd, using his pony to keep the herd together while he worked his way up toward the scene of the trouble.

But the new kid, riding sweep, ignored the herd. As soon as he saw that maverick longhorn bust out of the brush, he pounded his heels into his pony and headed for it full-tilt, shaking out his lariat loop and yelling like a Rebel. The bull was a lean, tough old Texas veteran of the hard Wyoming winters, hell-bent on getting to the cows in the herd, and, if he wasn't stopped, he'd scatter the herd from hell to breakfast.

Wild-eyed steers began to break past Link, heading for open country. Cows bawled and plunged, rearing up to come down on the back of the cows near them, starting to mill in panic. Kyle clubbed at them with his quirt, forcing them back, pushing them into a mill, trying to keep the nervous ones with the bunch, keeping his pony between them and the oncoming bull.

Link and Kyle saw the kid racing at the bull, his loop whirling, ignoring the fact that this Texas maverick weighed more than his light pony, that to rope the frenzied bull would lead to horse, saddle, and man being dragged through the brush and arroyos. If they were lucky. Otherwise, the bull would pull the horse off its feet and attack both horse and rider with those deadly long horns.

"Look at that!" Kyle yelled through the noise to Link.

"Let the herd go! Get over there!" Link yelled back.

Two other riders, the Pinto Kid and Dick Elliot, had moved up from the drag and were working the flank of the herd, whacking animals with their coiled ropes to turn the whole plunging bunch to the left, forcing them gradually into a churning circle. Link and Kyle shook out loops and put their ponies into a gallop, trying to reach the kid, who rode at top speed to intercept the bull a hundred yards from the herd.

They said later they had never seen anything like it.

The new kid didn't slow his horse, or swerve. The bull saw him coming, but too late to turn and slash with his horns. The kid rode his horse full speed directly into the rear flank of the running bull, striking a glancing blow, and, as he went past, he dropped his loop neatly around the bull's near hind leg and kept on going.

Taken by surprise, the bull jerked his head around toward his attacker, felt something tangle around his hind leg, dragging it under the other leg. He swung his head forward again, but a horn tip caught in the grass, and he flipped over to come down hard on his side. His back was broken.

The new kid stopped his pony and turned back. He shook his loop loose without dismounting. He was sitting easy in the saddle, contemplating the bellowing, struggling animal when Link and Kyle came riding up. The bull kicked with his front legs, trying to stand, still challenging the horsemen with his great horns. His hind legs flopped around, useless. There was pain in the wild, rolling eyes.

Kyle looked back to make sure the other two riders had the herd moving, then fished around in his saddlebag and brought out his Colt. He dismounted and handed Link the reins of his pony, walked within a few feet of those dangerous horns, and shot the bull once right between the eyes.

The new kid sat there, waiting for his praise, as if he had just done the cleverest thing in the world, but Link only said—"Get back on your sweep."—and he and Kyle rode back to the herd together.

"Stupid kid," Kyle finally said, using the corner of his bandanna to wipe the inside of his eye patch.

"I suppose that bull was one of those Texas snakes Art bought to breed with Hereford stock," Link said. "Wonder if we'll ever see the last of them."

"Winter should've killed 'em off," Kyle said. "That poor ol' guy, though. All he wanted was some female company after a long, dry spell. He smelled cows and couldn't help himself. Headed straight for 'em."

"Well, he went and died for it."

"Must be a lesson in there."

"You made a clean shot of it," Link said. "Don't think the cattle even heard it. One shot, right in the head."

"Yeah," Kyle said, stuffing his bandanna back into his hip pocket. "Nice and clean. I hate to kill an animal for no reason. Damn' poor way to go, breakin' his back like that. Damn' kid would've sat there and watched him die slow."

"Nothin' else to do," Link observed.

"Yeah."

"Well, let's get this bunch straightened out and moving. Art said he'd have the buyers at Arapaho Creek by noon."

Kyle let his horse drift back into position beside the walking cattle. In each of the dark thickets along the route, however, he now saw ominous shadows and phantom movements and knew they would not look the same to him for many days to come. He glanced at the new kid, riding alone far off to the side, riding somewhat more slumped in the saddle. And he felt sorry for the kid's punishment. Whether what he did was right or wrong was of no matter; the foreman had not liked it, and so no rider would ride with the boy, or wave or smile to him, or speak to him unless it was absolutely necessary. For the next few days, the kid was an outcast.

Kyle and Link reined in their horses on top of the last knoll so the herd could catch up. The sun was hot, and the trail had been long, and the cattle now plugged along in a mindless kind of way. Far to the rear, the Pinto Kid and Dick Elliot kept them moving and occasionally rode up along the flank to head off some steer wandering away. The new kid was still on sweep, riding three times as far as the flankers because he had to go into all the side draws and investigate each swale and thicket for strays.

"Extra buggy," Kyle observed, looking down toward the big corrals on Arapaho Creek.

Link reached around in his saddlebag for the field glasses and had a look.

"Appears to be Gwen's. Got the sunshade rigged on it."

He handed the glasses to Kyle. It always seemed weird how Kyle would hold the field glasses up to his face, the one eyepiece pressed against his black leather eye patch.

"Yep. There she is. And here comes Art."

Art came cantering up, glad to see two of his best men looking calm and relaxed, glad to see the herd in the distance just walking peacefully along. It meant that things were fine and the exchange should go nice and easy.

" 'Mornin', boys."

"Art."

"Any trouble?"

"Nah," Link said. "Got 'em full of good grass and plenty of water, and they just came walking along like a bunch of school kids. One of your wild Texas steers tried to start a stampede a while back."

"Oh?"

"New kid roped him. Broke his back. Then this ol' deadly marksman here"—he nodded at Kyle—"put him down with one shot. Between the eyes."

Art looked at the herd, still a quarter mile away, then looked back beyond it as if trying to see the place where the last of his great longhorn experiment probably lay dead in the grass. He gave a kind of sigh and turned back toward the corrals.

"Well, the buyer wants a good tally. I figure to have his boys take about a third of the herd around that knoll over there and lead 'em into the farthest corral. You boys take a third and head 'em to the second corral, and I'll take Dick and the new kid and we'll push the rest into the small corral. The buyer and his man can count while they go in the gates, if we don't rush 'em."

"Gotcha," Link said. "Is that the lady boss in the buggy there?" He grinned.

"You bet," Art said. "And she brought a friend, not to mention a picnic lunch. Get this herd corralled and we'll give you some coffee and sandwiches in the shade, how's that?"

Kyle swung his horse toward the herd and touched its shoulder with his quirt. "You coming?" he said.

Splitting the herd took no time at all. Art and the buyer agreed on the count, signed the papers, and the thing was done.

A welcome little breeze came drifting along, gently flapping the fringe on the buggy awning. In the shade of the only cottonwood for miles around, near the corner of the smaller corral, Gwen made a small fire of twigs in an old fire ring and set the blue granite coffee boiler over it. Her friend came up with a small armload of twigs and branches and dropped them on the pile next to the fire ring.

"Here come more of your husband's cowboys!" she said. The boys had dismounted next to the corral to slap the dust from their shirts and chaps.

"And no two alike." Gwen smiled sweetly.

"I'll say not! Let's see . . . we have one very handsome one, with a fierce black mustache. . . ."

"Link," Gwen volunteered, opening her picnic box to find the can of coffee.

". . . and one who wears a fancy vest and lots of silver doodads on his hat and belt. . . ."

Gwen looked up. "Oh. They call him the Pinto Kid. I can't imagine why."

"Who's the other one . . . the one with the eye patch? He could be quite good-looking if he weren't scowling."

"That's Kyle Owen," Gwen said. "A very nice boy. Well, a man, actually. We nearly lost him a couple of years ago when he rode into the mountains and didn't come back. Art and some of the boys finally found him, and he had become very savage, very deadly. He's still moody at times. Certainly not the sweet young man he used to be. There was a woman behind it, I was told."

"Oh?" her friend asked.

"Very strange woman. She inherited an irrigation scheme and somehow got Kyle to be her gunman and protect it for her. He was there, oh, just over two years. Maybe more."

The men stood clustered together like schoolboys at a church social, each one waiting for someone to move toward the females. Even the kid who had rode full-tilt into a crazed range bull and the lanky wrangler who shot that bull between the eyes were hanging back, shy of getting too close to those skirts.

Art and the buyer walked on over to the fire and made themselves comfortable, cross-legged, on the ground. The cowboys took this as a sign there was no danger and came closer. Dick and the new kid got there first and overheard the other woman talking to Gwen.

"Oh," she said. "There's no milk for the coffee. I quite like milk in my coffee."

Gwen laughed. "And isn't it odd," she said cheerfully, "here we are with a hundred cows a stone's throw away, and no milk!"

Her laugh was delightful.

Dick and the new kid looked at each other. Two minds, both somewhat numbed by the presence of two very pretty females, sharing a single thought.

"Get your rope," Dick said. "Ma'am . . . uh . . . Missus Pendragon?"

"Yes, Dick?" She smiled.

"If you can give us a few minutes . . . maybe loan us your pail. . . ."

"Why! Thank you, Dick! How sweet!"

Gwen spread a grain sack in the back of her buggy and dumped the oats onto it, then handed the pail to Dick. He stopped at his horse for his lariat and climbed into the corral where the new kid was already moving among the cattle, looking for one who had a calf and was still carrying a full udder.

"Here's one!" he called. The range cow looked at him with mild interest and started walking away to be with her companions when she felt the rope around her neck. Before she knew it, she was up against the fence with her neck tied firmly to a rail. The kid was young and impetuous, but he had handled milk cows before. And Dick, why he'd milked cows on the farm as soon as he was old enough to walk. Dick moved in with the pail, cooing soothing words to the wild-eyed cow. He didn't stop to think how much he looked like a slinking prairie wolf, crouched over and moving slyly toward her flank.

"Want some hobbles?" the new kid asked.

"Nah!" Dick said. "This won't take that long. Just need a few squirts is all."

At the first touch, the cow brought up a hind leg and shot out with it, sending the human prairie wolf flying in one direction and the clanging shiny thing flying the other. Suddenly another animal had her around the neck, and still another one was trying to twist her tail off. She stood stockstill, waiting for the right moment.

The one with the pail came at her again, keeping himself low back where she couldn't see him. The one gripping her tail said something. The other one grabbed at her udder again.

The right moment had come. One hind foot shot out and connected with something soft that grunted and squealed. She twisted, kicked forward, heard a clanging noise and another pained yell, kicked with the other hoof just in case something was sneaking up on the other side, but that got her leg tangled on the rail and she couldn't get it down. In panic, she wrenched against the rope and plunged with her forehoofs. The rail cracked and went down, and she was free.

The way the group standing at the buggy saw it was this: one bowlegged cowboy squatted down next to a wild range cow while two other cowboys tried to hold her, and she kicked one in the crotch, sent the second one flying halfway to the next corral, followed by the bucket, and finally busted down the rail she was tied to. She jumped the bottom rail and headed for high country, dragging along the new kid still hanging to his best rope for all he was worth.

Gwen stood there, hand on heart, watching the boy go bouncing through the sage at the end of the rope. "Link!" she cried, "help him!"

Art turned, thinking to see Link in the saddle and closer to the corral, since there should be some reason Gwen called out to the foreman rather than to him. But Link was on foot, running for his horse. *Better him than me,* Art thought. He should have told them the folly of milking a range cow in the first place.

Link swung his horse away from the corral and went pounding after the running cow, getting a loop ready as he went. The sound of the horse's hoofs faded into the distance, and quiet returned. Soon there was only the shuffling of the livestock and the crackle of the twigs in Gwen's small fire.

Kyle walked quietly over to his own horse and took something from the saddlebag. On his way back, he unfolded his clasp knife and punched two holes in the thing in his hands. The two women were now seated on a blanket in the shade, the lunch hamper next to them along with the coffee pot. He handed Gwen the little can of condensed milk with the red label.

"This is easier than milkin' a range cow," he explained. "Y' just go in th' store and ask for it."

Gwen laughed. "Kyle, I'd like you to meet my friend Julia Connelly. We were schoolgirls together. Please . . . sit down."

Kyle sat down on the grass next to the blanket, being careful about his dusty Levi's and spurs, and accepted a sandwich and a mug of coffee.

"Couldn't have been too long ago. Since you were schoolgirls, I mean."

Julia Connelly studied the man a moment, taking in the tan face, the lean torso with big shoulders, the eye patch. Even encumbered by spurs and stiff chaps he sat cross-legged on the grass as easily and with as much poise as another man might sit on a Chippendale chair. And in the few words he spoke she caught the tiniest hint of a lilt.

"Now," she said, "my Irish granny would call that the

blarney!" Her own smile caused dimples beneath apple-like cheek bones. Her eyes sparkled. "Would you be from an Irish family, I'm thinking."

Kyle's index finger went up to wipe at the edge of the eye patch, a gesture he made involuntarily whenever confronted with a challenge.

"American born," he said. "But my folks was Irish."

Julia Connelly offered a plate of sliced cucumbers seasoned with vinegar. She smiled at having made the cowboy say even that much about himself.

Art joined them, helping himself to the sandwiches, and pointed off beyond the corral. "Your cow milkers are coming back," he said.

Link was riding toward the corral, leading the cow on his lariat. Far behind him, they saw a small figure walking. Julia reached for the little can with the red label and added more to her coffee. "You're right, Mister Kyle," she said. "This does seem easier!"

The buyer joined them, his men fixing their own lunch over by his buggy. Link sat down just off the edge of the blanket, as Kyle had done, but directly across from the two women to have a better vantage point. As for the other Keystone hands, they were more than happy to walk past the hamper, one at a time, and receive a plate of hefty beef sandwiches and cucumbers and a mug of coffee from the hand of Gwen Pendragon, who served them without rising.

"Now come back for more," she said to them, "and later we have a melon and some pie Mary sent out with us."

"Yes, ma'am." And they went to sit in the shade of the Keystone buggy where they could eat without the embarrassment of trying to hold polite conversation at the same time, even though the conversation consisted largely of Art and the buyer discussing the condition of the range, the price of cattle, the problems of getting good help, and early signs of a hot summer coming.

Julia Connelly helped Gwen slice and serve the melon and the pie, and afterward the cowboys sought out what shade they could and stretched out with hats over faces, "nooning," as they called it on the range. Link stayed to talk with Art and the buyer—or to spend more time in the company of Gwen Pendragon—and Julia asked Kyle if he wouldn't like to take a walk up the next knoll, "to find a bit of a breeze, possibly."

Seeing the lean cowboy in chaps and Stetson walking with the pretty young woman in her wide straw hat as they strolled toward the soft rise of ground, one might imagine them to be deep in questions and answers. The day being warm, they went very slowly, sometimes having to step away from each other to walk around a cactus, sometimes going single file between the yucca plants. She paused from time to time to pluck tiny yellow flowers or to pick up and examine a shiny pebble; he would pause, too, watching her, and in spite of his normally somber countenance an admiring smile kept crinkling at the side of his mouth.

Kyle took out his clasp knife and cut a long yucca bayonet, stripping the fibers of it just to give his fingers something to do while he walked. He saw her looking at a single high cloud in the sky, all puffed and white, and then they looked at each other and smiled. A light wind from out on the sage flats stirred Kyle's chaps, swirled Julia's skirts, and smoothed her hair back from her face. They stood looking at the rangeland spread out before them.

"And Art owns all this?" she asked.

"Well, sort of," Kyle said. "Some is in his name, some in Gwen's. Missus Pendragon, I mean. A lot of it's open range, meanin' the Keystone don't own it but grazes cattle on it. Keystone owns most of the water, which is the important thing."

"Clear to those mountains?" She was looking at the sweep of purple ridges far to the west.

"Yeah, in some places the Keystone runs clear up there. Mostly for the wood. Partly for water. We got an irrigation ditch comin' out of the hills, for the hayfields."

"I imagine the mountains are beautiful," she said.

Kyle's eye narrowed and his smile went away as he looked toward those mountains, remembering only the killing and the killing and the killing he had seen there. The killing he had done there. He remembered the woman who had used him for a guard dog and who somehow kept driving him to rage. It seemed long ago, and it seemed like a bad dream.

"Yeah," he said, "there's some real pretty spots up there. It's cooler up there, at least. Me, I'd just as soon find a shady cottonwood grove down here on the flats, maybe with a spring runnin' through it."

"That's lovely!" Julia said. "You see, you do have the Irish poetry in your soul."

It wasn't anything like poetry. He knew that. But if it was she who said so, she with the dimpling corners to her mouth and cheek bones like the blush on a new apple, who was Kyle Owen to argue?

They stood on the knoll a long while, each with a hundred questions, but neither wanting to break the quiet peace that lay all around them. A pronghorn loped through the sage in front of them, and Kyle raised his arm to point, his long heavy quirt dangling from the wrist. Julia started to look, but her attention was arrested by the quirt. Not because it was long and heavy, but because where the handle met the lash a gold ring, like a wedding ring, had been woven into the braid.

When Kyle lowered his arm again, her eyes went back to the pronghorn, and they both watched until the animal was out of sight. They looked at each other and smiled. No words.

Too soon, back behind them, she saw the movement of Gwen waving her shawl. The Keystone party was packing up to return to the ranch.

"I guess Gwen is ready to go," Julia said.

"Yep, I guess she is," Kyle replied.

Their walk back down the slope, however, was no less of an amble than their walk up the hill had been. Julia picked up a small deer antler, three shiny pebbles, a piece of an Indian arrowhead, and a feather she thought might be an eagle's. Kyle Owen returned with the memory, a slow-turning kaleidoscope of remembered sensations fresh as that day's sun and old as the human race. He had been given a reminder that there are gentle women in the world, women who do not practice manipulation, women to whom any setting, even a bit of bare ground rising from the prairie, offer numberless small causes for joy.

Chapter Two

THE RIDER WITH THE QUIRT

"Where's the new kid?" Sam asked, looking over the cowboys gathered at the porch for Art's morning instructions. The sun was just over the horizon, and the sky was a transparent blue. On the shaded side of the big house the air still had a little chill to it, but they could tell from the look of the sky that it was going to be another hot, dry day.

"I sent him to bring in the horse herd," Link said. "A couple of you can start your day rubbin' some of the green off the string. There's some as haven't been ridden in a month."

"Rubbin' the green off" involved catching and saddling a dozen or more horses in succession, and riding each one in turn while they burned off their energy by kicking and bucking. It was a matter of getting them to settle down and remember that they were supposed to be working ranch ponies. The rider ended up feeling like his teeth had been jarred loose along with his brain. Besides a rider, two or three other hands were needed to hold the animals and saddle them. It was not hard work, but it could get exciting.

The cowboys eyed each other, trying to pick up on any signals that another man was interested, figuring to volunteer if someone else did. A man liked to choose his partner carefully for horse-busting, a man he knew and trusted. Standing there eyeing one another and waiting for someone else to go first, they looked like the stag line at a schoolhouse social.

Art came out on the porch with his big black ledger book.

No one ever saw what was in that book, but most mornings and on all pay days he would open it up and frown at the pages, then make careful notes in it. To some cowboys he must have seemed like God on Judgment Day, putting down their names and their sins in his book, ciphering up how their good points weighed against the bad ones.

"Where's the new kid?" he asked.

"Sent him for the string," Link said. As acting foreman, he also stood on the steps of the porch two steps higher than the cowboys, one step lower than Art. Art would give him the day's instructions, and he would parcel them out to the hands as he saw fit.

"All right. First off, the ladies are goin' into town to stay a couple of days. They'll need the best buggy greased and a good horse hitched to it. And while he's at it, have Pat check that bay we had on the wagon the other day. Seemed to have a gimp in one leg."

Link nodded.

"Next, Link, I'm wantin' you to go along to town with Gwen and Julia and see a couple of people for me. And we want to order salt blocks and barb wire, too. Choose a man t' go along with you, and line up a *segundo* to boss the crew while you're gone. OK. Get a couple of men workin' with the horse string so that gets done. Better get some men started on that barn project we talked about."

Art made some notes in his ledger, and closed it.

"Everythin' all right with you boys? Nobody sick or hurtin'?" It was Art's way of asking for advice, complaints, anything that might affect the efficiency of the group. And it was not a mere gesture—he held to the belief that every man on his payroll had to be free to talk up.

"Art?"

"Yeah, Lem?"

"I was out ridin' fence the other day, down on the south corner. Somebody cut the fence an' fixed it, an' that makes half a dozen times. Dang' wire is gettin' to be nuthin' but splices down there."

"Reckon who it is?"

"I figure it's just that lady nester out there, cuttin' through the corner. Her or one of her boys. Saves 'em two, three miles of ridin'."

"Can't be doin' any damage, if they splice it," Art said. "Tell you what . . . you take the new kid down there and build a couple of gates. I heard he's kinda wild with a rope . . . let's teach 'im the fine points of usin' fence pliers. Anything else?"

Silence. Art went back inside, and Link took over.

"All right, we're burning daylight here. Kyle, you're going to town with me and the ladies. Bob, as soon as the new kid gets in with the horse herd, you might cut out my string and Kyle's first. Put them in the calf corral. We'll need to pick which ones to ride to town."

Bob and Lem headed for the horse corrals, chaps flapping with each dusty step.

"Now. Kid," Link said, speaking to the Pinto Kid, "you're going to be the work crew *segundo* while I'm gone. You take five, six men down to the old log barn and put them to work shoring it up. They might have to go up into the hills and get some timbers. But we want it braced good in case we get another hard winter. Next, send somebody to see if we can't cut that new timothy down along Skunk Creek. Art thinks it's a bad, long winter comin' at us, and he wants every last bit of feed and bedding cut and stored somewhere."

"Then what'll I do?" the Pinto Kid said, grinning. Taking over the foreman duties would keep him moving from breakfast till sunset.

Kyle grinned and spoke up. "Do what Link does," he said, "hang around the kitchen, eat pie, drink coffee, take a nap. Oh, and don't forget t' spend a couple hours puttin' a crease in your pants and ironin' your shirt real pretty."

"Pretty funny, Kyle." Link scowled. "Maybe you'd like to lend a hand stringin' barb wire, instead of going to town?" Link turned to the Pinto Kid again. "After you check on how Lem and the new kid are getting along with their gate, drop over to see how the boys are doing with the horse herd. It should be noon by then. Then you oughta look at the irrigation up on the high hayfield and go down in the yearling herd and cut out any cows that are still suckin' a calf. Just don't try to milk them!"

The three laughed, remembering what a circus it had been the day that range cow busted through the corral rail and dragged the new kid right along with her. As if the memory had conjured up the victim himself, the new kid came walking up to the group, dusting his chaps with his hat.

"What's goin' on?" he asked.

"Well," Kyle said, a twinkle in his eye, "we just drew lots to see who got to go into town with the ladies and who got to go get into a wrasslin' contest with a couple o' rods of barb wire. Seein' as you weren't around, I drew your straw for y'."

"Oh," the kid said innocently. "Thanks!"

"Don't thank me," Kyle said. "You lost. Git your gloves and go with Lem."

The buggy and the two riders following had traveled less than five miles from the Keystone when Link announced they would stop to water the horses at the Rocky Creek crossing, just ahead. Kyle hid his surprise. *One more thing,* he thought.

First there had been the horses.

Every man on the Keystone had his own string in the horse herd, anywhere from six to a dozen mounts he used for his work. One horse would be good with cattle in a corral, another one better at moving cattle along on a drive; some were spirited and quick, others were steady and dependable. That morning Link had ordered his string and Kyle's brought into the corral, and while Kyle had chosen his "long distance" horse—a comfortable bay with a nice smooth gait—Link had chosen his "light" horse. It was a pretty little mare, deep chestnut. She was so gentle that she was almost a pet and could be ridden by kids, women, or anyone. Gwen often borrowed her for pleasure riding.

But for going into town, Kyle would have expected Link to choose more of a show-off, maybe that big white gelding with the high head and good muscles. Men and women on the streets of town respect a man on a horse like that.

Then there were the ladies. Kyle had seen Gwen heading off for town before, always in a nice dress and hat. Today she and Julia Connelly wore prim white shirtwaists with silk bows at the throat and soft silk vests. But he also couldn't help noticing that the skirts were split for riding. Well, he figured, maybe the split skirts were more comfortable for the long buggy ride, and they were carrying town dresses in the leather case. It looked like they had a lunch hamper along, too.

Finally, he didn't know why he was going with them. Link could handle the buying, and there sure hadn't been any trouble in the territory, not that would need two men. With gun or fists, Link was more than a match for any three men. And Gwen generally carried a pistol with her and was a good shot. Well, Kyle wasn't about to argue about it. A day of riding with two lovely women, a couple of nights in town, a long ride back—easy way to earn his pay.

At the creek crossing, Link let the buggy horse drink while the ladies stepped down to stretch. Kyle moved up— he and Link had been riding well behind the buggy so their dust wouldn't drift over the ladies—and let his horse put its head to the water.

"Link," Gwen said sweetly, coming to stroke one gloved hand across the rump of his mare, "Julia was saying she might like to ride a while. Could one of you men switch places with her, do you think?"

The thing was obvious, and quickly done. Julia Connelly in riding skirt and broad-brimmed hat took the mare. Link, hardly hiding his pleasure, took his place on the buggy seat beside Gwen. He clicked his tongue at the buggy horse, and they were off.

Kyle started to follow, but Julia stopped.

"Would you mind," she said, with that little lilt in her voice, "would you mind adjusting these stirrups for me? I'm afraid they're a bit long."

Kyle looked at the buggy, already getting smaller against the open range horizon, and dismounted to fix the stirrups. By the time he was aboard his horse again, the buggy was a quarter mile ahead of them. He was content to let the horses walk at a natural pace, knowing they would eventually overtake the buggy.

It was a warm day, and there was enough air movement to make it comfortable. In all respects it was a peaceful, sun-washed morning. Peaceful, that is, before the coyote dodged out of the little draw to their right, running toward a distant rise in an easy, swinging lope.

"Look!" Julia cried, pointing to it.

Kyle looked, but at her. He had seen coyotes before, What he had not seen before, certainly not within arm's reach, were such large and brilliant light brown eyes flashing in excitement. He had never been so near such red-brown waterfalls of sweptback soft hair cascading under the broad brim of a riding hat. Her hair tossed as she turned her head back and forth to look first at the coyote and then at Kyle.

"Come on!" she said, putting her heels to the little mare.

Kyle could not help but follow—out of the wagon road ruts, into the brush—his horse throwing sand and dirt as it caught up with Link's mare.

"You'll never catch it!" he shouted, but he smiled; she was already riding at top speed, smacking the ends of the reins across the mare's rump, now glancing back to see if Kyle was there, now leaning forward to watch the coyote, reminding Kyle of a kettle boiling on a hot stove with its lid dancing and bouncing in every direction. He brought the quirt down on his horse's hindquarters to catch up.

"We'll be a lord and lady!" she cried, burring the r, "on a foxhunt we are, taaraa taaraa!"

Wherever it was that coyote had gone to school, his lessons hadn't included anything about being the guest of honor at a foxhunt. And so, rather than running in a good straight line for a faraway burrow and giving the pursuing riders a fair chance at catching him, he took the first left-hand arroyo he came to, made a quick right, and vanished.

The two riders pounded on past the arroyo, the one with the softly flying red-brown hair still giving voice to her excitement, the other one, with his Stetson pulled low enough to touch a black eye patch, grinning at her and not caring where the hell the coyote was. They reined up, having lost all track of the animal, and found themselves quite a way from the wagon road. But Kyle knew the road; it took a long curve ahead of them, and so, if they rode due east, they'd pick it up again, probably within sight of the buggy.

"What a ride!" she beamed. "What a good little mare this is!"

"She just about outran me, for sure," Kyle fibbed.

"I need a riding quirt, though," she said, "like yours. Not so heavy. Where did you buy it? In town? I'd love to take one home with me, a real souvenir of the West."

"Made this one," he said. "We got plenty of time on our hands, come winter." He took it off his wrist and passed it over to her. It was surprisingly heavy. "Loaded with birdshot," he said. "Y' fill the handle with it. Makes a kind of club out of it, just in case."

"Oh, like a good old shillelagh!" Julia said. "And what's this gold ring doing on it?"

"Just a ring. A man generally has a *concho* or some kind of gee-gaw he braids into his work. The Kid has a quirt with jinglebobs on it."

"Jinglebobs?"

"Little bells, like. You might have seen some on men's spurs."

"Oh, I've seen those!" she said, handing him the quirt. "Perhaps I'll find a bored cowboy to make me a lady-size quirt with jinglebobs on it."

"Wouldn't be hard," Kyle said. "Finding a man to do it, I mean."

The glow was upon Julia Connelly, and the shine sparkled from her eyes as they rode along together. The rising wind kept grabbing at her hat, so she wore it slung behind her on its string, and her hair shone in the sunlight. She was still bubbling like that kettle lid, full of leading questions a young lady asks of a young man in such situations.

Yes, he enjoyed being a cowpuncher. Well, mostly he liked it because it got him outdoors and because of the good men he got to work with. Yes, he had lived other places, starting with New York when he was small, but mostly out West. He doubted he'd ever go back to the East again. Of family, he had a parent, his mother, still living and in the care of a brother who remained with her in New York. And a brother in the U.S. Cavalry. Father? Oh, a usual sort of story. Poor shanty Irish, went to England at fourteen to look for work, got caught stealing, and was sent to Australia. Three years. Made it to San Francisco after that and went to work putting telegraph poles across the whole country.

His own ambition? Well, at first he was after becoming a big rancher, so as to send for his mother and father and they'd all live on the easy street. Not to be. Then the father died, and the brother found a fine living as a foreman in a brickyard, and the mother was content to be in the old neighborhood with her old friends.

The pair rode up a hill and, looking down the other side, saw the buggy, still small in the distance, rolling along the wagon road. They would not catch up with it for an hour, at least, which contented them both. Quite well, in fact.

They paused. Julia accepted a sip of water from Kyle's canteen—although Link's full canteen was hanging at her knee. Oh, as for herself? Her large brown eyes seemed to laugh right into his one good eye, but with more cheery mischief than malice. Well, she was certainly born far above a shanty Irishman! Father is a big merchant in Belfast, thank you, and sent her to a good school in America. Wasn't it there she met Gwen, who was to marry the powerful rancher from the territories? But, and she flipped her fine flowing hair, as she said it, and dusted her riding skirt

31

with a gloved hand as if dismissing all the Wyoming soil from her presence, there would be no rancher for her. They are altogether too serious.

Kyle pushed his hat back, letting a few stray curls escape unnoticed, and wiped his brow with his bandanna. Then he wiped the inside of his eye patch.

"I'm thinking," he said, unaware of falling into her speech pattern, "I ought to tell you a story."

"If you must," she said, with her eyes smiling. Then: "Look! Aren't those deer? No, over there!" She had, indeed, pointed out a small herd of mule deer. They looked out of place there in pronghorn country.

"What is this story?"

"My father used to tell us about Ireland," Kyle said. "Mind you, he left there at fourteen and never made his way back again. But the story goes that the Owenses had broad lands, once upon a time, and even a castle."

"*Humph,*" Julia Connelly sniffed. "No doubt. A Welsh name such as that, with a castle in Ireland."

"Anyway," Kyle went on, "he knew his Latin, and his father before him was a gentleman who could read and who owned a large house. Before him, the Owenses had their own servants. Now, here's the queer part of the story. Back in New York, Father and me were walkin' in the park one day, me only a tiny shaver, and a fine-dressed gentleman with the Irish accent begins to starin' at us. Finally, he comes over . . . we were takin' a rest on a bench . . . and starts in to tellin' my father how I look like an old Irish family he knew. Aristocrats they were! Said I had the same cut to my nose and angle to my neck, same chin and all."

"Well, your features are rather . . ."—Julia put a hand over her giggle—"distinctive."

"And they were Owenses, so there. Not only that, but

one of that family, a woman my father and this gent took to be a great-aunt or something, brought a fortune of the family money out West and disappeared. The Irish gent said, though, that if I ever went West and ran into her, she would know me, and I would know her by our looks. What do y' think o' that, then?"

Julia Connelly sniffed and held her diminutive nose in the air. "I wouldn't call it blarney," she said, with that twinkle in her eye. "But when you go to make up a story, you should know to put in the details your listeners want to hear."

Kyle frowned at her. "What details?"

"Well," she said, "a person would be wanting to know about your life later on. About your poor eye. And where that gold ring came from, as well."

No pleasing some people, Kyle thought as they jogged along toward the buggy, the sun warm and the breezes whipping his horse's mane. He was smiling to himself. Silently he repeated her name. *Julia Connelly. Julia Connelly.* She made him smile all the way down inside. But he remained silent about the "details."

Chapter Three

THE BLACKSMITH'S RIDDLE

Link and Kyle escorted the ladies to the hotel before heading toward the livery with the horses.

"I'm goin' over to the mercantile to arrange for barbed wire, first thing," Link said. "Why don't you take the buggy to the smithy? He's got a keg of ready-mades we need to haul back to the ranch. Then go get yourself a drink, and I'll be there directly."

Kyle nodded. Good thing Link had brought him along to do all this work. One man to order some rolls of wire, and one to tell the blacksmith to load a keg of horseshoes into the buggy. If Link was alone in town, it would take him maybe an hour to do both jobs. If he stopped to talk for a half hour at each place, that is.

Kyle smiled about it. Old Link was about as obvious as the city slicker in that painting, hanging in the saloon. In the picture the slick-looking dude is bent down helping a girl get her boot heel out of a knothole. But anybody could clearly see that he was only doing it so he could feel her ankle and look down the front of her dress. All chivalrous and polite on the surface.

Link obviously wanted to be alone with Gwen, and not just so he could protect her from range bums and wild steers and rattlesnakes. But the friend from the East was in the way, so they brought along another man to keep her occupied. Kyle was of two minds about the deal. It made him uncomfortable to see these two making eyes at each other, but on the other hand it seemed pretty harmless. Gwen liked to get out and do things, and Art was busy all the time, and Link was just a good friend to talk to. And when everything was said and done, it wasn't any of Kyle's business anyway.

Whatever reason they had for bringing him along, it was a world better than stringing barbed wire or busting horses. Julia Connelly was more fun than a kitten chasing grasshoppers.

The forge was blowing sparks when he walked into the dark shed, and, as Kyle's eyes became used to the dim light, he made out the lanky boy pumping furiously at the bellows, making the long handle go up and down like he was being whipped. The big-shouldered man standing at the anvil wasn't the blacksmith. At least it wasn't John Peters, the town smith and farrier.

The man turned, red face rouged with soot and sweat, arms bulging under the coarse shirt, chest swelling the leather apron.

"Keystone Ranch," Kyle explained. "S'posed t' pick up a barrel of ready-mades."

"The Keystone! That's a long way to carry them even if you could pick them up!"

No, the big booming voice did not belong to Peters, the town blacksmith. But Kyle knew instantly who this man was. The voice in the gloom of the shed was that of the itinerant blacksmith. It was the man who wandered the territories with two wagons and an inexhaustible wineskin, the smith who showed up every season somewhere on the Keystone range and who vanished as mysteriously as he came. The blacksmith who drifted from place to place, always working at his unfinished iron chain, forever adding new links to it.

"The buggy's out there." Kyle smiled, jerking his thumb toward the livery stable.

The smith put down his hammer and growled to the apprentice boy that he could quit pumping the bellows. Then to Kyle's amazement, he gripped a full keg of horseshoes by the top and bottom chines and hoisted it to his shoulder. It would take two average men to lift that much dead weight, yet the smith strode out the door with it as if it were a sack of flour.

Kyle returned to the forge with him to sign the bill.

"John Peters not here?" Kyle said.

"Gone to wiving!"

The smith grinned in a way that suggested he had personally sent Peters off to some predetermined fate.

"Gone all the way to Missouri to bring back his bride. He's been writing to her for, oh, three years or more. We were in the area . . ."—he indicated the boy sitting on a pile of coal, and the silent woman on the old rocker far in a dusky corner, sewing—"and I said I'd watch the forge while he was away. Name is Evan Thompson."

The two men shook hands. "We met before," Kyle said.

"Yes. We did." The smith went around behind the great bellows and took down the wineskin and the two cups. He poured without asking, and handed one to Kyle.

"Changes coming for you," he remarked to Kyle, and it was not a question but a simple statement of fact. "And it's time. Here's your health!"

"Oh?"

"You'll see." The big blacksmith pushed back his skullcap. There was a strip of white flesh where neither soot nor sun had darkened him. "You were going west, last time I saw you."

"I went quite a ways west, as it turned out," Kyle said. "Won't be goin' that way again."

"Not if you're careful."

"No."

"You're going the other way first," he said, pointing eastward.

"Back East? Not likely," Kyle answered.

But the huge sooty man laughed his great laugh and swallowed a large draught of his wine.

"You are a case, One-Eye," he laughed. "You need to learn. . . ." He paused. "Life is . . . well, never mind."

Evan Thompson picked up a heavy chain link, an oval as long as a man's forearm and wider than the span of his hand.

"I meant you'll be going down the street." He chuckled. "Before you took your travel to the west, you were more than curious about the future. Down there . . ."—he pointed with his cup—"may be your answers. A fortune-teller came to town last week, set up her tent in the vacant lot next to the lawyer's office. You'll see her. She'll tell you your future, good or bad. Maybe both."

Kyle looked at the heavy link in Thompson's hand.

"What do you think of it?" said the smith. "You recall my showing you how to forge horseshoes. This boy . . ."—he pointed to the apprentice—"this boy isn't so quick a learner as you. What do think of his work?"

He handed the link to Kyle, and Kyle looked it over carefully.

"Looks fine to me," he said. "I can see the weld here at the end, but it's a smooth one, and a good one. Should hold just fine."

"You Keystone men." The blacksmith shook his head. "You make my work so hard at times. Look again!!"

Kyle studied the link. He ran his fingers along it, feeling for any place where the metal might be too thin or too thick, or flawed in some way. He banged it against one of the posts and listened to the ringing, in case it might tell him something about the temper of the steel. Or the iron. Hard to tell. Finally he handed it back.

"You got me," he said. "What's wrong with it?"

"It's good metal," the blacksmith said, ignoring the question, "and welded across the end of the link, not at the side, for strength. It's a lapped-over weld, too. Strong link, well-formed. One thing wrong with it."

Kyle set his cup down on the workbench.

"Promised I'd meet a man for a beer," he said, "so I'll have t' play at riddles with you another time. Thanks for loadin' the keg."

"Fare well," Evan Thompson said, splitting it into two words, like a benediction. "Maybe the fortune-teller will know the answer!"

In late afternoon in summer, when the day's small breeze has finally given up trying to cool the earth against the blazing prairie sun and a few hours before the evening whiffs and gusts take up the challenge, the whole world seems to be roasting. People come out of doors from buildings that feel like ovens, and they stand on porches squinting into the brightness, without moving, finally going back in where at least it is shady. Dogs and cats and chickens hunt out dusty ways to crawl beneath buildings.

The tent took up all the shade in the vacant lot beside the lawyer's office. From across the street, Kyle smiled at the incongruity. Three different signs hanging on the front of the law office proclaimed:

Attorney at Law

Marriage Licenses and Wills

Legal Contracts

Real Estate

Eggs & Oats Bought and Sold

The tent, in plain white canvas, bore a sign over the door that read:

Christollomay—Clairvoyant and Prognosticator

Contact the Deceased

Know Your Fate

Palm Reading and Fortunes Told

It wasn't anything but another fortune-teller, Kyle told himself. One of them came to the Keystone one Christmas and read everybody's palms. He had told Kyle he would be going on a long sea voyage, which, of course, he didn't. Still, it was something to do. Maybe he'd try it now, and he'd get Julia to try it later on. There wasn't much entertainment in town anyway.

Kyle hitched up his belt and adjusted his Stetson and crossed the street.

Madame Christollomay was sitting alone in her tent behind a large table draped with fringed black cloth. The air was perfumed and cool for the time of day.

Kyle let the tent flap fall closed behind him. She gestured to a chair opposite her, and he removed his hat and sat down.

"I thought maybe you'd be able to tell me if I'm ever gonna get my own place," he began, but Madame Christollomay raised her hand to silence him.

A long and awkward moment passed before she spoke: "The blacksmith set you a riddle," she said.

"Yeah," Kyle responded, "and it ain't the first time he's done that to me. Maybe you know the answer?"

"Of course, I do," she said. "But you have to find it yourself. Show me your palm."

Kyle held out his hand, palm up, on the table. The woman frowned, touching the center of his palm with her index finger.

"There is much written here," she said, "but it is not clear. Perhaps to touch the palm with metal would bring out the words. Gold would be best."

Kyle didn't need to have a stove shovel bent over his head before he got the point. He fished out a silver dollar and laid it in his palm.

"Silver," she said, taking it with obvious disdain. "Not as good. Perhaps more will be required."

"And, perhaps, we'll see," said Kyle.

"You are a singular young man," she began, which could refer to anything from his having just one eye to him being alone at the moment instead of drinking with a crew of cowboys. No surprises, so far.

"You will be making a long ride soon," she said. Kyle would be surprised if he didn't, since, if he didn't ride back to the Keystone, he'd have to take up residence in town.

"And there is a woman. A new woman." Now, that was a puzzler. Then, again, she might have figured that out from the way he looked. He had worn his new scarf for the ride into town, and his best gabardine vest and California trousers. He had also taken time at the livery stable to wash his face and comb his hair.

"Wait! Wait!" The fortune-teller became agitated. She reached under the table and brought out a large glass ball. "Place your hand on this, on the top of it, so." Kyle spread his fingers across the top of the globe. The woman stared into it, either worried over what she saw or putting on a very good act.

"I see you riding east," she said, her voice changed now, "yet a woman comes. From the west."

"Y' must have your crystal ball sittin' backwards," Kyle said. "It's the new girl who's from the East, and the ranch is west of here."

"Not a new woman. A woman you already know."

All right, Kyle thought, so she had spotted the gold ring decorating his quirt.

"Very, very strange," she continued. "Are you ill?"

"Me? No. Why?"

"You are Irish?"

It was a statement more than a question, and, of course, it was another easy guess, given Kyle's looks and the slight traces of brogue in his speech.

"The woman is in white. The crystal is not showing me everything," she said. "There is a woman, you are riding east, alone, and a female pursues you."

"What kind of female? Ridin' a horse, trying to catch me, is that what you mean?" Kyle's sense of amusement was starting to fade.

"That is not clear, at least not to me. Perhaps to you. I know little of these Irish things. I am Bohemian."

"What things are you talkin' about?"

"The woman who pursues. She is not altogether human. I know little of these things, but my belief is that she is a banshee. But the banshee chases only those who are dying, does she not?"

"Banshees?" Kyle said. "Don't know much about them. Those the same ones that howl and scream around at night when somebody's about to die?"

"Yes," the fortune-teller replied. "Very dangerous."

Madame Christollomay gazed into Kyle's face for a moment, and then, as though shaking off a disturbing thought, regained her composure and took Kyle's hand again.

"Your life line is long, but threatened. Often threatened. I do not see material things here, no sign of great wealth. Oh!"

"What?" These sudden exclamations of hers were starting to make him fidgety.

"How did you wound this hand?"

Kyle looked. "Never did. Got a dandy scar on this other one here, from a piece of barbed wire. Don't remember ever cutting myself on the other hand, though."

"I have never seen this," she said, staring into his palm. "This life line. Point your index finger north, thus . . . do you see how this line clearly goes east? But here it stops, and then here it continues. Yet there is no injury, no scar, no reason for the break in the line."

"Meanin' what?"

"Meaning you are more of a riddle than that posed by the blacksmith. You will leave a woman, and a woman . . . another . . . will follow. She will make you travel toward the east, but will not follow. A spirit woman, perhaps a banshee, will chase and hound you . . . and finally you will die, but you will not die. It seems you will be buried but not dead. I cannot explain it. I have not seen this before."

Kyle fished out another silver dollar and laid it on the table. "So what would you do about it, if you were me?" he said.

"Solve the smith's riddle. No one can tell you the answer, but you must find it for yourself. Only if you solve his riddle will you be at peace. If I were you, and thought I could avoid my fate, which one cannot do, I would return to my friends and stay among them, no matter what. No matter what happened, I would not leave. No matter what! Perhaps, after a year, after two years, perhaps all of this will change."

Kyle thanked her, told her he might see her again next time into town, and tried to put on a casual sort of air as he left her tent, like he was a cowboy come to town for some sport and some fun who could look up his pals and have a drink and laugh about what the fortune-teller had said. He moved off toward the saloon. No pals around, but he could sure use that drink.

Gwen and Julia spent a happy afternoon shopping for things necessary and things not so necessary. By day's end, they had seen everything in the mercantile store, the small hat shop down the street, and the local seamstress' tiny showroom of ginghams, laces, and a few extravagant rolls of silks.

Toward sundown they called on a family Gwen knew, and accepted their supper invitation with mixed feelings. It would be nice to sit down at a proper family table in a nice home, and neither of them had looked forward to dining at the smoky, hot hotel dining room—the only decent place in town for ladies. Yet at the public dining room they would have been with Link and Kyle.

And those two lords of the range, having loaded the

buggy, spent a couple of hours in the saloon, exchanging range gossip with the men, then wandered the streets, looking for Gwen and Julia. Toward dusk they gave up looking and posted themselves on a butt-polished bench outside the mercantile to wait. But when the dark came creeping to the edge of the little town, they gave up waiting and retreated again to the lamplight of the saloon where familiar male faces welcomed them to the card table and the whisky bottle. As for spending time with the women, there was always tomorrow.

Chapter Four

COMES A PALE RIDER

Mid-morning. The sun, uncomfortably warm, glared down on the Keystone home ranch. For the moment, the big ranch house and the yard behind it were empty, deserted, waiting.

One small breeze born behind some far-off scrap of sage came along through the brush and grass like a small boy kicking his way to school, sending up miniature dust storms, flailing the grass seed, bending tall stems. It meandered to the draped wagon sheets and peeked under, kicking up the edge of the canvas. Screened behind white canvas, in the L of the big house, a dozen tables stood expectantly. Ropes rigged overhead supported canvas awning.

The vagrant breeze flipped a few tablecloths, and then left the house, wandering down toward the creek behind the bunkhouse to send shivers along the white hides of five naked cowboys taking serious baths. A dozen cowboys in long johns squatted on the bank, combing their hair and brushing their clothes. There would be women at the afternoon social, "gen-u-wine" unattached single women.

Other Keystone Ranch residents were taking sensible naps, whether in the bunkhouse or in the big house or under shady cottonwoods. Saving energy for the party.

The party was for Julia Connelly, Gwen's very pretty friend, who was going away. Gwen sent riders with invitations to all the neighboring ranches. She arranged for musicians. A plank dance floor was put together, and neighbors were coming from miles away—bringing single daughters and spinster aunts—and the festivities would literally last until dawn.

Far west of the Keystone, a lone rider broke out of the foothill timber, going fast. A quarter of an hour later, two more riders came out of the trees, following.

Noon crawled to its zenith. More small breezes came skipping across the range and paused curiously at the Keystone's main house to tug at the canvas windscreen and awnings before going on. Two more hours dragged by. Then Gwen Pendragon, aristocratic in her white dress and upswept hair, came around the long porch to inspect the arrangements. She smoothed the tablecloths that the breeze had rumpled.

As if Gwen's appearance on the porch were a signal, buggies and wagons began showing up. Vehicle after vehicle came down the road, stopped at the porch to unload women and hampers, then went on to the stables. The women loaded the tables with covered dishes; pie appeared, cloaked in cheesecloth, and platters of cornbread and biscuits under oilcloth; watermelons and jugs of cider bobbed in the horse tank against the shadiest wall. Deep oval dishes of baked beans and chili crowded next to bowls of potato salad, applesauce, and plates of cold fried chicken. A fire pit outside the canvas drapes sent the succulent scent of roasting beef drifting over the whole ranch.

To the west, the fleeing rider from the mountains kept up a horse-killing pace, heading straight through the brush and leaping arroyos or recklessly plunging down one side and up the other. The two who followed were more cautious, but no less determined.

The sun moved toward the mountains; the crowd of people grew until the ranch buzzed with conversations, children played tag and hide-and-seek among the stables and barns, and scrubbed cowboys, sporting fresh haircuts, stood or hunkered around in little groups, admiring the younger ladies. Some of the canvas walls had been tied back out of the way, since the mischievous breezes turned out to be harmless.

The centerpiece of the party was Julia Connelly with her glowing reddish-brown hair and dancing amber eyes, who sat in a chair on the porch receiving a string of well-wishers and new-found friends.

Waiting deliberately at the end of the line so he could have more time with her came cowboy Kyle Owen in a fresh boiled shirt and sharp-creased California trousers. New haircut—white skin at the hairline meeting the deep working tan where his hat would normally be. And, of course, the eye patch slanting across his brow.

The running horse and its rider, coming in from the west, gave the startling appearance of being a single entity; the horse was so light-colored that it looked yellow, and the woman in the saddle wore a dress of pale yellow, nearly white, leaning low over the horse's neck as it ran.

The pursuing riders were mounted on dark horses. But when the buildings of the big Keystone Ranch came into view on the horizon, they began to consider veering off.

Julia indicated that Kyle should sit in the chair next to hers. Kyle had not been so content with life, so thoroughly infused with utter satisfaction, in many years. All of his past seemed a mere fog, a hazed blur of some other place and some other time, belonging to some other man. Sometimes in his dreams he would remember a woman for whom he had killed men and savagely beaten others. Sometimes he would hear a phrase or see a certain object of some kind, and he would stop instantly to stare off into empty air, his mind seeing himself in that past life like looking through a stereopticon.

He sure didn't want Julia to go, but knew she had to. And he was grateful for the hours she had spent with him. Ever since they had ridden to town and back, he felt eager to get on with making a life for himself, to work toward some kind of future. Like the fortune-teller, he couldn't see many details and had no idea where he was going to start, but when he looked at her, he knew that he was going to.

She held out her hand to him, and he took it.

"I shall be missing our rides, and our walks," she said. "I wish I could stay and see the fall colors . . . and the winter. Winter must be beautiful at times."

Could be, Kyle thought, *with the right person. With a woman like Julia Connelly to exclaim over each ice crystal, each yellow leaf.*

"Gets pretty bad," Kyle said. "Those fall colors don't look like they do back East. Just one or two colors of yellow in the aspen."

"Still, we could find glorious places, couldn't we?" she said.

"Yeah," he said, "but you wouldn't like a week-long blizzard out here. Nothin' to break the wind, and it piles the snow up somethin' fierce. We spend a lot of time in the bunkhouse, playin' cards."

"And weaving ropes and reins, you told me," she said.

"You *will* remember to make me a quirt, won't you? A nice light one, for a lady."

"I'll remember," he said. And thought: *But when it's done, you'll have to come back here to get it.*

The moment arrived, and both of them knew it, to bring up the subject of letter writing. When a single woman and a single man agreed to exchange letters, it was tantamount to a prelude to an engagement. Kyle could taste the tension in the back of his throat.

Several people saw the rider coming hard, and the word spread quickly. A crowd gathered at the front porch as the woman came dashing through the front gate. Art Pendragon called for men to come and take care of her horse while Gwen urged her to dismount and take refreshment, but the slightly built, pale young woman remained in the saddle, breathing hard, while studying the assembled guests.

Kyle Owen knew who she was.

He was standing on the edge of the porch, almost within reach. She fixed him with her eyes.

"The ring," she said. She said nothing more. No one knew what she meant, or why she kept looking at Kyle.

He knew. Luned.

He excused his way through the knot of people and strode quickly to the bunkhouse, returning with his heavy quirt. Without a word, the pale woman in yellow accepted it and studied the way he had braided the wedding ring into the strips of leather.

Kyle stood at her stirrup as if in a trance. Three terrible years swept through his brain like a horrifying dream.

"This man," she finally said, addressing those that had gathered, "does not deserve to live among you. Your Keystone Ranch is known throughout this territory for fairness, for helping those who need it, yet this man . . ."—she pointed at him with the quirt, and the people could see the gold ring shining on it—"this man came to Crannog, murdered our foreman, took over his place, his belongings, and became the guardian of our mistress. She agreed to marry him and to give him equal shares . . . more than equal shares . . . in the irrigation project. But he left us to our enemies. We had no protection against those who came to ruin the ditch. We had no one to oversee the workers."

The Keystone guests were silent. Somewhere back of the ranch house there were children shouting and playing, but the crowd at the front porch was silent.

Art Pendragon had at first been struck speechless by this pale apparition showing up on his front step to rage about one of his riders. But when she stopped to catch her breath, he stepped in.

"Now, just you hold on there. When we came to your place and found Kyle, he didn't even remember who he was, like somebody had doped him with something. He wasn't the same man as when he left here. And if he married anybody, it's because he was out of his head somehow. He's not the same man we knew, but, at least, he's not the same as the one who did all that killing up there. There was another man he was up there lookin' for, and maybe it was him that did all this. You're welcome to light down, and we'll make you welcome as long as you want to stay, but you can't go attacking my men."

"This Keystone ranch of yours is said to have respect for women," the woman fired back, "yet you let this deceiver live here. My mistress wears black. Her livelihood is threatened. I defended this man of yours, I told her he would return. But she accused me of being the one who drove him away. It is only because of me that she waited three years, getting more bitter each day. And it was I, a woman, who continued to defend the project. A woman! There was a small boy, and he and I were the only ones to stand against the destroyers. I killed two of them and had to flee, afraid for my life. There are riders chasing me to bring me back. Or kill me . . . or worse. And all the fault of this man. This man does not deserve to live! *This* is what I think of him!"

She drew back her arm and cut Kyle across the face with the quirt, and the blow nearly knocked him to the ground. Before anyone could do anything, she wheeled the pale horse and raced away, going out through the gate and turning eastward.

Kyle put his hand to the fiery red welt across his face and started toward the bunkhouse. The solemn crowd parted to make way for him, and no one spoke. Gwen's hand unconsciously found Julia's and gripped it as they stood shoulder to shoulder, dumbfounded.

Kyle took his hat, his Winchester and Colt, his saddlebags and his coat, and saddled his horse. He moved in a trance, his mind seething with thoughts that would not connect. His face burned. Julia leaving, hating him. Luned had lied. He wasn't really married to that woman. Gwen's party all spoiled. What was Art saying? Art would be. . . . And he couldn't look at Gwen. Back to Crannog? No, that was over, too. He seemed frozen to death, unable to think what to do, feeling his strength ebb away. There was only one thing to do. His hands performed automatically, tightening the cinch, buckling the bridle, tying down the saddlebags, and rolling his coat to tie behind the cantle. Automatically, coldly, Kyle Owen got into the saddle and headed off. He took a road alongside the hay fields, and then the flats of native grass. He opened the last gate and rode into the sage.

This part of the range looked dead and empty and lifeless. He rode with the sun hot on his back, and many eyes watching. He rode slouched and staring ahead with his one good eye.

He neither knew nor cared where he was bound. His mind went back to Crannog, to the killings and the beatings. Crannog lay far west and north of the Keystone Ranch; Kyle Owen followed his own slumped, plodding shadow eastward.

It was getting on toward dark when Kyle came across a youngster riding toward him on a plow horse. The boy recognized the Keystone brand and had heard descriptions of the one-eyed cowboy. Kyle figured the kid was one of the Irish woman's boys, the woman who had bought the old Everitt place with the log house on it.

"Mother would be havin' ye to supper," the youth stated.

Kyle nodded and went with him.

The woman was glad to have a visitor from the Keystone, glad for a chance to repay the Pendragons' kindness. Why, the Mrs. Pendragon herself had sent a rider just a week ago to ask them to a party, although with the work and all they couldn't make it. And hadn't her boys been cutting the fence to take the short cut to the plowed field, and didn't she see with her own eyes two Keystone men coming and putting in gates for them?

Familiar with the hospitality customs of the high plains, Kyle expressed appreciation over "a real home-cooked meal" and praised the coffee. After supper, he said he'd best be going on so he could find a spot to camp before it got any darker. The woman looked out the narrow window.

"Wind comin' up," she said. "The stable's clean and

dry, if you'd care to stop there for the night. Such a wind would likely keep ye wakeful all the blessed night long, lyin' out there on the plains."

But it was not the Wyoming wind, whistling and puffing through the gaps in the walls of crooked cottonwood logs, that kept him from sound sleep. It was violent dreams of an irrigation ditch high in the mountains far away, of men buried in shallow graves, blood on the rocks and sand. It was swirling thoughts, images flying around inside his head like they were caught in a tornado, Julia's face whipping past him, then those of the men he had killed or beaten, then the porch of the ranch house and the crowd of people standing, watching him, then a quirt cracking across his face, a fortune-teller in black shawl, staring at his palm, then another vision of Julia.

He twisted and rolled one way and the other in the saddle blanket laid on the straw, and by dawn's first light he was curled up tight and shivering from the air plucking at his sweat-damp shirt.

One of the Irish boys came with coffee and found the one-eyed man sitting in the straw, staring straight ahead. He was in a daze as he straightened his clothing and combed his hair, and he was not much company at the fine breakfast the woman set before him. Fine it was, with fresh mush and berry syrup for it, and four fried eggs laid on top of a generous slab of fried scrapple. Kyle could not find it in him to make conversation, beyond compliments of the food, but he was thinking that he could stay in such a place. Just be a sodbuster, milk a couple of cows, live out his life inside the four secure walls of a little dug-out.

Not here, though. Too near the Keystone. He could say he'd stay and work for his keep, even build his own dug-out or shanty to live in, help her and the boys build up a good farm, but they would come from the Keystone and take him away, just as before. And he could not go through it again.

Kyle could not refuse when the older boy wanted to take him to see all the improvements they had made on the place, and so it was mid-morning as he made his good byes and praised the woman's cooking—for the tenth time—and climbed up into the saddle to head east. What lay in that direction, for him, he did not know.

Nightfall found him far from any habitation, and so he slept his twisting, tortured sleep out on the prairie under the shelter of a shallow arroyo bank, but around noon he came to a lonely farmstead and was offered midday dinner. So he traveled on, slowly, slouched in the saddle, taking shelter in abandoned soddies or at any windbreak offering itself, accepting jerky from a wandering hide hunter, or a meal from a discouraged woman being taken west in a dilapidated covered wagon.

He went on and on, sometimes veering to the north and back again to the south because he had seen some bluff or butte. Such landmarks seemed to have meaning to him, but he did not remember. The creeks he crossed were still running, this late in the season, and, when he found one, he would stop and sit beside it, or camp beside it, staring at how the water flowed along. Sometimes he tossed sticks upstream and dimly tried to figure how long it would take them to pass him.

Kyle had spent three years at the source of a river, at the immense ditch that brought the river's life-giving waters from the mountains above timberline to the farms lying below the foothills. He had known a woman of vision, a woman with the single-minded purpose of making and keeping the ditch, of bringing that water down. But they had come for him, Art and the Kid, and Pasque and Will, and at the Keystone he'd realized it was no good to live up there without the company of men, even in a grand house and with a fortune waiting to be made in water. It was no good, living just for himself, not trusting anybody, not really knowing anybody. Getting up every day and going out with a gun to seek those who would destroy the ditch, and having no other reason to get out of bed. A man needed a job where he could do real work, where people needed him. A man needed to work alongside men he knew and trusted.

Art had brought him back to the Keystone and back to life, but Lady Fontana's woman had come riding into the ranch and ruined everything again.

The man with the eye patch sat beside a trickling stream, lost in the plains somewhere on the east edge of the vast Wyoming Territory. Or he was in Nebraska, for all he knew. He only sat. His back was slumped and his face was grave and his mind was a staring blur. The water gurgled in the grass, the setting sun blazed hot on his back, and a north wind rose to tug at his coat.

Chapter Five

GOING UNDERGROUND

He was still traveling as summer gave way to autumn. Chokecherries turned deep dark red, and wild plums went from pale to rich purple. He ate on these and whatever game he could shoot, mostly rabbit and sage hen. The knee-high grass became yellow and crisp, and the cottonwood leaves dried so that the wind rattled them. He found the thick, short stems of Indian breadroot and dug up the roots and peeled them, chewing on them as he rode.

Nights were growing cold.

Sometimes he stopped at homesteads and accepted hand-outs and shelter, claiming to be "riding the grub line," although his wandering tracks took him far from anything like real cattle ranches. Some settlers knew about the custom of a cowboy riding from ranch to ranch, saying he was looking for work and glad to get a meal, but when they looked at Kyle's torn hat and ripped shirt, his bleary eye and unshaven face, they did not believe he was after a job. Most of them took him for a drunk, a range bum.

The day of the first snow found him beside a sandy riverbed so wide he could not see across it. Days before that, and he didn't care how many, he'd crossed a good road and hurried to hide himself as a stage went jangling by, a crowded coach pulled by six horses, and figured it might be the line to Deadwood. He didn't care, except that lonely stage stations sometimes let a man swamp out the stables for a meal.

He sat the horse, looking at this new riverbed as if it were a problem. Might be the North Platte. Might be he'd drifted so far east, it was the Platte itself. Snow flying on a whistling wind swirled around him, twisting the horse's tail toward its flanks, stinging Kyle's neck and ears. Some of it caught on yucca plants and powdered the sandy ground in the lee of cactus or sage. This was a dry snow, too dry to stick to his dirty coat and scratched-up chaps. It came from behind and flew past him on both sides, then converged into a white scud, and he couldn't see a stone's throw ahead. Kyle urged the horse down over the riverbank, and they slowly felt their way through the clumps of willows half obscured by blowing snow. After a few hundred yards he came to running water and stopped and contemplated it. Then he rode on in, the water coming up to the horse's knees, and they came to another hundred yards of empty sand sprouting islands of willow where driftwood had snagged. Must be the North Platte. Didn't matter.

That night, the face of the fortune-teller came in his dream. The blacksmith came, too, holding out the heavy link of chain to him. Both of them were trying to warn him, tell him something, and, for all of his tossing back and forth and moaning in his half sleep, Kyle could not shake off a picture of himself riding through an empty riverbed obscured in swirling snow, crossing shallow water, and going on.

By morning the snow was several inches deep, and deeper in the little hollows where the whistling north wind had deposited it, but the sun rose in a flawlessly blue sky, and some grudging warmth returned. Kyle walked to warm himself, letting the horse follow if it wanted to, and not caring if it did. He gnawed a leg of rabbit saved from the last time he had built a fire. Three days? He'd found it in the pocket of his chaps. Then, coming over a rise and seeing nothing ahead of him but rolling prairie hills powdered with snow, snow and prairie stretching clear out to those far-off bluffs, he knew what he must do.

It brightened him a little, this sudden sense of purpose. He mounted the horse and rode toward those bluffs, watching the ground for signs of game. He found them, tracks and fresh droppings where a few deer had grazed that morning. He followed. With that old familiar cool efficiency of killing, he selected one—a doe, plump, looking over her shoulder at the horseman with huge curious eyes—and shot her. He cleaned out the guts, left the head, strapped the carcass behind his saddle by tying the legs together underneath the horse, and turned back toward the bluffs.

"Cold this morning," he said to the horse. He was surprised to hear himself speaking, and he plodded along, thinking about it. They came to a place under a cottonwood where green grass showed, and he stopped to let the horse eat.

"Have to hole up pretty soon," he said aloud. But he was not talking to the horse now; he was talking to the woman, to Julia Connelly. All these days he had been carrying her with him, and now he had begun to talk to her.

"Winters get pretty mean out here," he said. "We'll be all right, though. Get us a place built, over there. East side of the bluff. Sun keeps the snow melted there, and there's shelter from the wind. North wind, mostly, around here."

He hauled up the horse's head and started on again, still talking to her.

"Get us some food laid in, like this deer here. Jerk some meat, gather up plums, Indian root, and stuff. We'll be all right. Need firewood, too. And tools . . . gotta get tools somewhere. I'll take care of it."

A long string of dirty hair blew across his eye, so he raised the ragged hat and pushed it back over his ears out of the way. He combed his dirty fingers through his beard and thought about what else it would take to live out here.

They did not reach the bluffs that day, but, along toward noon of the next, the white and brown land began to rise like a frozen sea swell and the bluffs looked not as high as before. Riding down through a shallow draw timbered with crooked cottonwood and dwarfed cedar, he lost sight of the bluff altogether. With only a couple of hours of daylight left, he came to the unexpected. The bluff was a half mile away, but at his feet there was a prairie cañon nearly fifty feet deep, a broad and twisting slit in the earth running as far as he could see in either direction. The edge was abrupt. He could see it had caved off recently, and he kept the horse away from it.

He rode first one direction, and then the other, looking for a way down, or a way around, but found none. Far below them, a little stream of running water seemed to mock at them, for both man and horse were thirsty.

"Dry camp tonight," he said to the woman he carried in his mind. "Tomorrow we'll find a way across. These arroyos sometimes go on for miles, but there's always a way across. Buffalo trail down to the water, maybe."

He staked out the horse and took elaborate care in laying out his saddle blanket and the scarred saddlebags, as if he were setting up a whole camp outfit for her. He told her to wait while he scouted for supper. He took the rifle and went creeping through the brush. Before long an unfortunate jack rabbit hopped out in front of him and made the mistake of freezing, instead of running. The ragged man wiped the inside of his eye patch with one dirty finger and proudly carried the rabbit back to the blanket.

"This'll do," he said, "once we get a fire goin'." He gutted it and hacked the head off, and hung the carcass to bleed while he looked for firewood. He made a circuit around in the brush, muttering and snapping off dry branches.

"Not that greasewood," he said to her as if she were helping, "that'll make it taste terrible. Git some of that sage, there. Git that big dead cedar branch."

He got down on his knees and used a flat stone to dig a shallow pit. He built a fire in it, and, when it had burned down to coals, he buried the rabbit there in its skin. By the time darkness fell, the meat was edible.

"Dry camp," he repeated, wiping rabbit grease on his chaps. "Get some water tomorrow." Then he broke the last rabbit leg in half and winked slyly while putting the pieces in his chaps' pocket.

In the cold of morning he left the horse to graze and walked farther down the rim of the cañon. Seeing how the water down there twisted its way through the soft sandstone maze, he thought of the Crannog irrigation project and of Fontana, and he spoke to her.

"It'd take more than we got t' get that water up here," he said. " 'Course, a man could dam the whole cañon and fill it like a lake. Start a new project, right here, 'cept your big house, it'd look outta place."

Like an animal that expects to be hunted, Kyle looked not just down at the cañon but all around him, and he stopped when he saw something strange far out in the sage, away from the deep notch in the earth. Too far away to tell, but it looked like a building. He returned to camp and saddled the horse and rode there. He went cautiously, mumbling to himself, or to Fontana, or to the horse. Julia was no longer there.

"Somebody here," he whispered hoarsely. "Guess I was just sayin' the word house, and one shows up. We'll ease up on it, real quiet now. *Shhhh. . . .*"

He wiped a finger under his eye patch and loosened the Colt in its holster, which had shrunk and warped tight to the gun, but there was no need. The house turned out to be nothing but some poor sodbuster's shack. He could see where a big garden had been grubbed out of the sage and yucca, but all that remained were drifted dunes of loose dirt. The building had walls of crooked cottonwood logs, mud-chinked, but the chinking was dried up and falling out. Whoever had built it had tried to make a roof of sod laid over poles, but the poles had broken and sagged to the earth and the sod was a mound on the floor.

Out in the bush was a privy of sorts, and near it the remains of a lean-to. Here the sod roof was laid over shorter, thicker poles, and so it still gave shade and shelter to the rattlers and spiders living in it.

Kyle poked around in the wreckage, lifting his head every once in a while to sniff the air as if he expected the owner to come back. He kept the horse with him, the reins looped in his belt, just in case.

"Look-a here," he said to the horse, suddenly stopping to pull at a pile of rotten posts and rusting wire. "Part of a shovel." There was no handle, the rivets hung uselessly from the socket, and the blade was cracked up the middle. "Not much, but maybe we could use it," he said, tying it behind the saddle. Deeper in the pile he came to an iron rod, flat on one end like a pry bar, and a rusted bucket with the bottom caved in, and these he also tied onto the saddle. Another hour of searching turned up nothing more of use to him, nothing but fence posts and bent nails, the skeletons of rusted-away tin cans. He picked up an old stove leg and stood there with the breeze whipping his shaggy hair and beard, weighing it in his hand, holding it this way and that like it could make a tool, or weapon, and with his one good eye he studied the design embossed in the metal as if reading there some wisdom of ancient people. In the end he tossed it away.

By riding a diagonal route back to the cañon, he found a way down, a place where animals had worn a trail to the water.

"Found it," he said to Fontana, urging the horse down into the cañon. "Now we'd oughta go upstream an' look for grass and wood. And a place t' dig in for the winter." Fontana was not there to answer him, but the dry north wind cried around the sandstone ledges and echoed in the overhangs and followed him, whispering.

The place he chose was a rise of ground within the cañon, on the western side where the early morning sun would warm it. It was high enough to be safe from a flash flood, and he could see a long way up and down the cañon in both directions, in case somebody was coming. Nearby, a huge section of the high bank had caved off, leaving a mountain of dirt and brush. It would make a good place to take cover in case of a gunfight.

The horse could graze in the big flat pasture across the creek. Maybe he'd cut some grass up on the rim and toss it down into the cañon so he could store it somewhere for the months to come. He knew for sure he needed more provisions.

Only the jack rabbits and an occasional deer saw the ragged man going slyly about his preparations for winter, and many of the rabbits and a half dozen of the deer became jerked meat, their hides stretched and drying. He dug a crude cache into the side of the high dirt mound and soon had it full of dry meat. Indian breadroots also dried in the cache, along with wild rose hips and wild plums. When he found good stands of prairie grass, he harvested it and threw it down, covering it with dried deerskins. He broke off every dry cedar or mesquite branch he could carry and stored these under the cañon's overhang.

One day his foraging took him far from the cañon, a day's ride, almost back to the wide shallow river, where he heard the sound of shooting. He hid himself and the horse in a thicket and waited, and, after an hour of listening to the prairie silence, he ventured toward the source. He found the stage road, and two buffalo, one dead and one limping pathetically.

"Sports," he said to Fontana, his eye scowling down the road after the long-gone stagecoach. "Ride along on top o' the stage, shootin' anything they see along the way." He spit as a gesture of disgust. "Good for us," he said, dismounting. "I'll butcher this one and make a drag for the meat outta the hide. Then we'll maybe get after that other one."

He had never butchered a buffalo before, and, as many a plainsman found out, it is a tedious job when you don't know what you're doing. Just getting the hide exhausted him, rolling the heavy carcass back and forth. Severing the tendons and breaking the joints was ten times as hard as cutting up a steer. Dark overtook him at the task, and he heard the low-throated howls of prairie wolves far out in the sage.

"You get on back t' camp," he told the non-existent woman. "I'll stick it out here and keep the varmints off our meat. Be a long night."

He flopped the wet hide over the joints of meat and sat with his back against it, gun in hand. He figured he had five shots in the Colt, six or seven more in the gun belt. Didn't have any left in the saddlebag. But the thought of the saddlebag reminded him of the horse, which he caught up and tied next to the buffalo carcass.

The wolves knew to avoid the stage road and the smell of humans. Their ears picked up the sound of the crippled buffalo crashing in the sage, and they left Kyle to his kill to go after their own. All through the night Kyle listened to them, out there somewhere in the bush, snarling and barking over their kill. As soon as it was light, he finished cutting up the meat, piled the pieces onto the hide, attached his lariat to it, and began the long day of dragging it back to the cañon.

In the following days he made trip after trip to the sodbuster shack, using horse and rope to drag away all the usable poles and logs. He took a different route each time so as not to leave a deep trail. He threw the wood over the edge where later he would pile it under the overhang.

One day, prowling around for another place to hide wood, he found the sodbuster's cañon hide-out. It didn't surprise him much, because settlers were a scary bunch who took every dust swirl on the horizon to mean marauding Indians or a gang of outlaws or a tornado. They generally had a hole to hide in. He found it behind the mountain of dirt left from the cave-off of the cañon bank, a hewn timber sticking out of the rubble. He dug at it with the shovel until he found it attached to another beam. There had been a tunnel in the side of the cañon, and this part of it had broken off in the landslide. It didn't take long to find the rest of it. It was a shored-up, low tunnel just wide enough for a man, leading back into darkness. He made a couple of torches and went in. He had to crouch as he went.

The tunnel opened into a small man-made cave where he could stand upright. There was a keg full of some kind of grease, some dried-up harness, a rusty pickaxe, and a grain bucket. Pegs driven into the dirt wall held a heavy coat, thick with dust and gnawed by mice, a coil of wire, and a rotting nosebag.

The stage road and the ruined cabin had made him feel cautious and wary, but the sight of these human things was a fist grabbing his lungs. His skin went icy. He scrambled out of the tunnel as fast as he could go, splashed across the stream to the horse, and hid under the cañon overhang.

"Stay hid," he said, either to the horse or to Fontana. "People been here."

He slunk close to the bank, came to the trail, crept up it, stayed low in the brush, searching all around. For an hour he watched and listened, his hand sweaty on the Colt. Eventually he retreated to the tunnel. He went in, came out again. Went in again, scooped a wad of the grease and plastered it around the end of one of the torches, where it burned with a yellowish light. He grabbed the pickaxe, looked back to see if anyone had followed him out of the tunnel, and returned to the cañon.

"Listen," he said to Fontana, whispering. "They've been here, but I think they're gone. I'm gonna make sure they don't get down here."

If the woman were really there, she would have seen a dirty, long-haired, bearded figure hunching up the cañon, dragging his rope and the pickaxe. She'd have seen him crawl up the steep path to the lip of the cañon and loop the rope around a sagebrush trunk and then tie it to himself.

He began hacking away at the side of the cañon, undermining the thin sod, digging away until, with a *whoosh*, it all collapsed into an avalanche of dirt and sand and clumps of grass rumbling down in a choking cloud of silt. When the cloud cleared, he untied the looped rope and pulled it down with him as he dropped to the new pile of rubble.

The trail out of the cañon, the only trail he knew of, was gone. As he slumped back toward his tunnel, dragging rope and pickaxe, the wind came from behind him and followed him, moaning.

More snow came, laying its glaring silence like a white blanket over the sage country. The raggedy man in the bottom of the prairie cañon spent the mornings slicing and smoking his buffalo meat. He took shelter from the snow by creeping into the tunnel, a little farther back each time, until the human things no longer startled him. The cave became safe for him. He dug a food cache into one wall. It was easy digging.

He dug the settler's beams out of the rubble pile and used them to make a roof between the pile and the cañon wall. Carrying bucket after bucket of dirt out of the cave, he buried the roof. Finally he went far up the cañon where he dug bushes and small cedar trees to plant in the mound, and, when it was finished, his tunnel entrance was hidden from view. Anyone looking down into the gorge would see a high mound where the bank had collapsed, and they might see a gaunt horse that had somehow gotten trapped down there, but that is all they would see.

He kept on burrowing away, making another food cache to which he moved the dried roots and wild fruit, then making alcoves for the firewood, always carrying the dirt out in the bucket to dump it on the backside of the mound or to spread it out on the cañon floor. When more winter snows came, and the cold, he dug a narrow tunnel in the side of the cave, more of a crawl-way, and at the end of it he hollowed out a sleeping chamber. Just inside the chamber he dug out a little shelf for a fire and discovered the smoke would drift into the cave and then out the tunnel where it would dissipate in the air. He made a deep bed of dry grass so he could sleep warm even without a fire. The creek froze solid, so he brought ice and snow into the cave to melt for water. A wide shallow hole in the floor, lined with one of the stiff deer-hides, made a reservoir where he could crouch down and drink. Mercifully the perpetual gloom of the dark cave kept the water from showing him his reflection.

Chapter Six

"IN THE SOUL'S HAUNTED CELL"

GEORGE GORDON, LORD BYRON

As winter deepened, he stayed in the cave days at a time, sitting against the wall, staring into the gloom. Memories came, sluggish and bleary. Memories of long winters holed up on the DHS ranch or at one of the Two Bar line camps. The winter at Crannog, Fontana's huge house, haunted all other memories. At Crannog, as the cold deepened and deepened, the walls had closed in and the presence of the woman became a tightness running up his spine. When the walls of her house had become unbearable to him, he used to go riding, his body wrapped in layers of clothes and scraps of blankets under a sheepskin coat.

He shuffled down the tunnel and peered out into the frozen glare of the cañon, thinking he ought to go find the horse. But in the end he only went back inside to hunch over his fire.

More thoughts came, unnoticed, and slid away again without troubling him or causing much interest. He saw himself at Fontana's ditch, beating and killing that Army engineer, and let it pass. He saw himself and some girl on a breeze-scented hill, but it meant little. Hour after hour, scraps of the past floated by, and he made no effort to hold them. If no thoughts came, so much the better.

From time to time he shifted his position and sniffed the air. Memories meant little to him, but he took primitive pleasure in sniffing out the scents coming from his cave.

There were smells of dry clean earth, and damp earth.
Smells of his dried meat, smells of the sage and cedar wood
stacked in the dark niches, fresher smells of the roots
cached close to the bed, smells of the bed itself, smells of
the tiny stick fire. Sometimes a faint musk smell came from
nowhere, and he would raise his head and paw his hair back
from his ears to listen and sniff the air. Finally he would
curl up again and doze. The wind alone bothered his sleep,
howling at the mouth of the tunnel.

At times he would go exploring his burrow, dragging the
bucket and broken shovel to enlarge a tunnel or carve another hide-out hole. He liked doing it in the dark, quietly
digging and packing the dirt hard until he had a place large
enough to lie in, and then he liked to lie there, sleeping on
the fresh-smelling earth. In the blackness he thought about
the world outside his cave and would send his mind out the
tunnel and up the cañon side and across the sagebrush deep
with snow to watch the stagecoach go by, and then he
would nearly weep in the dark, feeling terrible pity for those
people. How busy they were, riding their coaches and their
wagons and their horses back and forth, back and forth,
taking themselves on such urgent journeys to make money
or beg for money, to find love or run from love, to look for
friends or visit the graves of friends lost. And the danger!
Those of the outside world, those poor wandering creatures, always guarding their money and guarding their
things and guarding their lives and even guarding their
thoughts from the other wanderers.

In this mood, pity would sometimes turn into a kind of
panic. He would come fully awake and stare into the blackness, mentally mapping his burrow and its tunnels and
hiding places and worrying that he had done it all wrong.
The food was too close to the tunnel, where some animal

might smell it and come inside to investigate; one of the woodpiles was in the cave where some intruder could set fire to it or use one of the thick cedar branches for a club. In this state of mind he planned traps that would fall on any man or animal crawling into the cave, then he worried about being caught in the trap himself. He planned blind tunnels to mislead intruders and figured out ways to wall up his storage places so they couldn't be seen. Once he scurried out of his sleeping hole and into the main cave, frantic with a sudden realization of how easily anyone could find and enter the cave from the smell of the smoke, if nothing else. Another time he thought of the horse: surely someone might find it and follow it back to him. The thought of it grabbed him like a giant fist until he fell down with his knees pulled up to his chest.

One day he stood inside the big room of his cave, one dirty finger busy wiping the inside of the eye patch, studying on an idea. He seized his shovel and began digging a hole, chest-high, on the opposite wall. It would be another sleeping place, except that from this one he could see anyone coming into the cave. They would be outlined against the dim light coming down the tunnel. When they stooped to look into his old sleeping burrow, he would be behind them. And then—his eye narrowed at his own craftiness—then, while they were trying to see into his old sleeping burrow, he could either stay where he was and hide, or attack them from the back. Or even escape through the tunnel.

He crawled into the fresh hole because he was tired, but long hours passed before he slept. The winter wind outside the tunnel whistled and cried and moaned, and each time it stopped it made him worry that someone was standing at the opening, blocking the sound.

A day came when the north wind stopped as abruptly as if someone had closed a door, and the sudden silence brought him awake. He groped in a niche for a chunk of dry meat and ate it, then took a grease torch and went crawling up and down his tunnels, feeling in the dark to make certain his food and wood and stacks of dry grass were undisturbed. He felt silly for being a coward, and the idea brought a grim smile to his cracked lips. No one knew where he was; no one cared. True, someone might find what was left of the homestead on the rim of the cañon and might even follow the tracks he had made to the edge, but they would see nothing. If they somehow caught the smell of the small fire, it would probably frighten them away. Out in this uninhabitable country, the only men who made fires were renegade Indians or law dodgers or maverick rustlers, men that only the worst kind of fool would go looking for. As for the horse, it was probably long gone, maybe no more than a rack of bones under a snowdrift somewhere.

He crawled up into his favorite tunnel, reaching into the small niches to take stock of his food supply and bits of firewood. The tunnel wasn't as good as the big room where he could stand upright, but it was nice to lie on his back, the ceiling within arm's reach, chewing a strip of dried rabbit. He thought he would build another sleeping place up at the end. He lay there, planning. Up there the wind wouldn't be so loud, when it came back.

And then he heard the sounds. Whimpering sounds. Scratching sounds. With his ear to the side of the tunnel, he could even hear crunching, as if an animal were chewing on bone. He recoiled in fright, crouching against the opposite side, furiously pulling at his long hair and holding the torch pointed at the other wall like a sword. The smudge drifted back down the tunnel behind him as if air was seeping through the very earth itself.

But sounds? How far could a sound carry underground?

He crawled back for his revolver, although he was unsure whether the few cartridges were any good. Back at the tunnel's ending, he made himself put away his fear, and he began to dig at the wall, pulling the dirt toward him and packing it under his knees. The sounds drew him upward, which was good; when he dug up toward the surface, it was easier to drag the dirt down. After he had extended the tunnel a few feet, less than a body length, he heard a bark, like an alarm, and then sounds of something hurrying away just as his shovel blade broke through into emptiness. A smell of musk poured through to him, and his torch flared with fresh air.

A coyote den. Deep and warm under the prairie, cozy with its bed of silt and fur and grass, still warm from the bodies of the animals. He saw two tunnels leading out of it, and one of them showed a bit of light. He crawled on, pushing the shovel ahead of him to enlarge the narrow places, sniffing the clean winter air coming down.

The coyotes had been clever builders—the tunnel came up under the roots of a wind-twisted, drought-dwarfed cedar growing in a soft, crumbly rock outcropping. The man crawled forward with infinite slowness, watching the hole above him for any sign of shadow moving, and listening for sounds of foot or hoof. Eventually he put his head out far enough to see the overhanging cedar and the crumbling rock, and he listened again. Hearing nothing, seeing nothing, he pushed himself up until his upper body was clear of the hole, and he looked around.

From the height of the rock outcrop he could see far away, almost to the stage road and the river. Off in that direction he figured out where the old homestead had been, and behind, the way he had come, he could see the long dark slit of the cañon. Feeling bolder, he climbed out and stood there, looking in all directions, shifting his gaze from time to time, like a man memorizing a place. The winter air was motionless and silent, and the only snow he saw was drifted in little patches behind the sage. It was a chance for him to get some more firewood, maybe do some hunting.

The newly discovered burrow became a fascination. He was proud of himself for finding it, even though he did not need any more tunnels to guard and even though it posed new dangers to his hiding place. Now there were two entrances, two places for strangers to discover. But it extended his domain and gave him a place to lie and study the whole area.

Just as the coyotes had done, he lay on the sun-warm rocks to scan the sage flats for game and signs of danger.

Hunting for a slab of stone to cover the den entrance, he explored a second rock outcrop. It was on a promontory where the cañon turned eastward. Here he could see all over the sage flats, and he could also see down into the cañon where his cave entrance was. He could see the other stone outcrop, where the den was. He sat down on the rocks, a lone figure of rags and hair perched on the windless sage-spotted prairie, staring down into a crack in the earth. Hours passed and the man grew chilled, but still he remained there, watching and watching.

He was guarding himself.

There came over him a warming, reassuring fancy: he was still in the cave, sleeping, at the same time he was guarding the entrances. This is what he had been searching for all that time—a way to be left alone and a way to have his supplies and himself protected, guarded by the one person he could trust. Himself.

In the following weeks of winter, whenever the wind was not blowing, he would rouse himself and crawl up through the coyote tunnel, dragging the deerskins he used for warmth, and go to the promontory to watch and guard his doorways. Sometimes, with a sly look in his eye, he would try to trick any watchers by shambling past the promontory a hundred yards, and then watching it as well. No one came, not an animal, not a man, but he planned how he would attack them if they did.

Sometimes the breeze brought the faraway sound of a stage driver cussing his teams along the Deadwood road, and sometimes the sound of a shot as some rooftop passenger threw lead at a jack rabbit or coyote. Then the man would rush to his tunnel and drop into it until just his head showed, peering under the cedar limbs. It would take hours, but the panic would pass away, and he would walk to the road to see if anything had been killed, and then he would creep back to the looking-over place and resume his vigil over his doorways and himself.

Sometimes he did not want to go back to the cave. Sometimes he recognized it as a deep, dark trap in which he could easily be caught. Other times he wanted to build a path down to it and put up a gate at the rim with his name on the gate, inviting people for a visit. But then he would remember how everyone was coming for him—Fontana, Luned, Art and the Keystone riders—and he would stay in the meager shadow of the sage and worry about tracks he might have left out on the flats. That fortune-teller had said a woman in white was coming to get him, was following him. He would have to be more careful about leaving tracks.

* * * * *

A wind came up one evening.

It was like no wind he had ever experienced. Sitting at his watching-place, chewing on roots and jerky, he heard a far-off moan. At first he thought of the stage road, since sometimes strange sounds came from there, and thought it might be the sound of wooden brake shoes on a runaway wagon, the ear-piercing screech as the wet wooden blocks were levered hard against the iron tires.

But this moaning came from the north and grew into a wail that made him cover his head with his arms. It rose in pitch and fell again. It chilled his spine. He looked up the cañon and saw some invisible force advancing, coming along and whipping the branches of the trees, bending the dry grass over, kicking up spurts of dust and sand. He watched it go past his cave entrance and on down the cañon, its voice fading.

Then he heard it again—again from the north—this time more of a deep-throated howl than a moan, and he saw dirt swirls rising in the air. He ran for the coyote tunnel and dropped into it, feet first, reaching back to struggle the stone slab into place. He did not think of torches or anything else, but only crawled as fast as possible for the cave. But the cave was choking full of flying dust and dark as any of his tunnels. The howl was inhuman and unbearable; he escaped up his favorite tunnel, the most comforting of his tunnels, and found dry meat in a niche and huddled with his knees drawn up to his chest, chewing for all he was worth on the meat, his free hand trying to cover his ears against the terrifying wail of the wind.

All night long it screamed and screamed, rising and falling. When a lull came, the silence seemed worse than the screeching, but then the wind-demon came back, louder than before, ripping at his eardrums. He wanted to get the shovel and collapse the tunnel down on his head, just to shut out the noise. He held both hands over his ears and howled back at it, raging at the wind until his throat was raw and his voice no more than a dry, dust-caked whisper against the terror.

The wind found the cave opening and shouldered its way inside, reaching for him, probing the tunnels for his body, howling at each niche and tunnel mouth. It came part way up the tunnel in which he crouched and screamed back at it, but then it found the tunnel to the coyote den and went there, instead, its howl turning to a whistle like a hundred locomotives gone berserk as it found the upper opening and burst out into the prairie night.

When the wind finally let up, he did not know how many hours or how many days had passed. The stillness and the cold woke him, and he crept to the cave door to find the sky a solid leaden gray mass pressing down on the plains and the air moist and chilling. He went back in and built up the small fire, and, when he felt a little warmer, he ventured outside and went up and down the cañon, gathering up limbs and bits of brush the wind had ripped up and tossed aside. He found himself looking for tracks; he could not get over the feeling that some kind of being had ridden in on that wind, some awful power. He thought of going up to his look-out to watch, in case it was lurking around either of the entrances, and discovered he was afraid of being so far from his cave. And so the lonely, shaggy figure retreated into his tunnel and curled up and slept, haunted by his dreams.

Winter in the sage plains east of the Rockies is nothing like winter in the northern and eastern states. On the high plains there often comes the "January thaw" when snow melts fast and the wind seems suspended. At times the thaw lasts so long and is so warm that small tips of green grass appear in the ground and buds start to swell on some of the bushes.

The screaming winds came several more times to the lonely cañon, each time heralded by the strange moaning breeze coming along ahead of it. Then the thaw began, and, although it was a false thaw and he had no faith that it was the beginning of spring, the man began to thaw, too, and peered carefully out his cave door. There was a grudging warmth in the air and in the sunlight striking the side of the cañon, and he was no longer afraid. He was not even afraid when he heard the yapping and howling of coyotes—or perhaps prairie wolves—up somewhere on the rim above him.

The sound reminded him of food. He went deep into one of the tunnels and felt around in the niches. Plenty of meat, but it wouldn't hurt to find more. There could never be enough. He crawled up into the coyote den and through the tunnel to the opening under the cedar tree, emerging into the bright winter sunlight like a badger with only one good eye blinking at the vast empty flats all around him.

Not far off, the coyotes were making a kill. They had jumped a lamed antelope, and some were jumping around yipping while others snapped at the flailing hoofs and bared their fangs against the animal's throat. The man moved toward them, but in their frenzy the coyotes did not see him. The antelope gave up its last terrified breath in a squeal and succumbed to the bloody jaws just as a bulky figure in flopping rags reared up out of the sagebrush, waving its arms and growling.

"*Waugh! Waurgh, hiy!*" it roared.

To the coyotes, it was nothing less than a grizzly. With

tails clamped down and lowered ears they made a dash for safety and stopped fifty yards out in the brush, suddenly free of their hunger for antelope, or at least for that particular antelope. The strange bear seized their prey by the horns and dragged it to the edge of the cañon, where he threw it down. And the bear vanished under the cedar growing from the rock outcrop.

It was a scene that was to be repeated frequently as long as the thaw lasted, even when the little skiffs of snow came on the freezing air. The upright predator, robed in rags and deerhides and smelling like six kinds of death, followed the coyotes and the wolves on their hunts, rushing at them to claim the remains of a jack rabbit or half of a bloody gopher. Once the pair of wolves caught a coyote far from its burrow and killed it, but were frightened off by the bear-like thing who wanted their prey. But neither the wolf pair nor the coyote family fled the region, for it was their territory. Instead, they grew accustomed to this strange new presence and seemed to accept it.

As for the man, he went out when he was not afraid and followed the *yips* and *yowls* of the hunts or wandered, looking for places where tracks of young antelope or deer were imprinted with canine footprints. He became adept at knowing the ways of the four-footed hunters and sometimes left part of a kill for them, carrying the rest to his cave to dry over a meager, smoky fire. Once a gopher invaded his stores, and he woke to hear it chewing, and he killed it with his hands and took it up the coyote tunnel and left it outside for them. The gift remained there two days before one of the coyotes was brave enough to creep up and retrieve it.

He did not neglect his wood caches during this thaw. He took squinty-eyed joy in surveying the cave room with its rack of drying meat strips and piles of twigs and branches too large to be stored back in any of the tunnel hideaways, which were already stuffed full of fuel and meat. He still worried about enemies finding him, especially in the freezing weather when he couldn't lie on the look-out rock and watch over his tunnel entrances. What he needed was a way to barricade those openings.

One day he remembered that he had hidden some of the homesteader's fence posts up the cañon, having used the horse to drag them to the edge where he had thrown them over and later stacked them in shallow undercuts at the base of the cañon wall.

Those logs. He was going to make them into a corral for the horse, but the horse had left him. Then he thought he might make a privy of some kind for Fontana, but she didn't seem to be with him any longer. But they would make a good thick door for his burrow.

So the man of hair and rags went out with a length of rope and dragged the posts back to his lair, one at a time, and fashioned them into a cumbersome barricade inside the tunnel. He wanted to make a real door and spent hours, squatting at the fire, staring at the pile of posts, trying to figure out how to make a door without bolts or wire or rope to fasten them together. All he could do, finally, was set two upright posts into deep holes, set apart, to hold horizontal timbers. To get out, he had to lift them up, one by one.

The moaning wind returned on a day when the air was full of frost. The places the thaw had opened on the creek were skimmed over with ice. The sky lowered, and he could not tell where the sun was. He felt the cold even inside his cave and wrapped his feet in an extra layer of deerhide and tied an extra hide over his back, bringing part of it up to make a hood. He planned to go get three more posts to finish his barricade, but the only ones left were a long way up the cañon.

The small wind came first, as it had done before, wailing like a woman in labor as it came crying down the cañon ahead of the storm. The ragged man bent into it, clutching the deerhide around himself. The sound grew and grew, and the wind was not attacking him so much as warning him, twisting around him with shrieks and alarms, waving arms over him. It seemed to fly over his head, sometimes sobbing, sometimes whispering. He twisted this way and that, trying to see it, but always it was only the shrill crying sound. Finally it went on past him, plucking at his deerhide in a final flurry like a hand desperate to have him follow it, and then all was silence and stillness in the cañon again. Nothing moved.

He hurried on up the cañon, knowing the main storm would soon be coming at him like a fast freight. He would just have time to get the posts and get back, and that would be all he would need. With those three posts, he thought as he shambled rapidly along, he could finish closing the opening. Then he would be able to sleep, able to let his guard down and enjoy the good food he had gathered. It had cost him many, many days and weeks, that food, catching it or stealing it from the animals, hacking it into strips or pounding it into pemmican and drying it by the smoky fire. He had a right to it, and it was all his. He had the right to enjoy it in the darkness, without the world coming to bother him. And with his barricade completed, just two or three more logs, he'd be where no one could get at him. Locked in with his supplies, he would finally be free. And safe.

When he got to the overhang and found the three old fence posts still where he had left them, he chortled in his beard. Once again he had foxed them, the invaders. He had their fence posts and everything else worth having from the homestead, and with his own ingenuity he had hidden them and covered the tracks. He looked up at the rim of the cañon, his one eye squinting like a sly thief about to make off with a bag of money.

Got them. His. He wrestled each one out of the frozen silt, wiggling them back and forth, and tugging, until he was damp with sweat. His hands were freezing, but he went on struggling, with numb fingers, to free the fence posts and get the rope wrapped around them so he could drag them down the cañon. Just these three, he chortled, just three, and he would be safe in his cave for the rest of his life. He would need nothing else, once these were in place.

He was halfway back to his tunnel when the storm hit the cañon. A great curling cornice of wind-driven snow—small dry ice particles at first—soared upward on the prairie's winter thermals and looked down at the slot in the earth. In the bottom of the slot, a strange ragged figure was tied by a long rope to three heavy posts, the rope around his shoulder, and he was moving with odd lurching, lunging motions, sideways, tugging the load along with him like a bear caught in a trap chained to a log. The mountain-high white cornice of freezing air and snow came to its maximum height and dropped like a hammer, slamming into the sage and earth and rising again in a million flying particles of sand and ice crystals. The fury entered the cañon and tore down it, gaining speed as it went, pushing white ice before it.

Then the larger, wetter flakes began. In a soft New England snow such as lithographers print on Christmas cards, the large wet flakes would fall softly like downy feathers or drifting milkweed seeds, gently covering the forests and

81

roadways with a blanket. But here in the dry frozen air of
eastern Wyoming with nothing larger than a cedar tree to
break the wind, the wet snow flew on the gale with such
speed and flurry that men would later find range cattle
frozen, still standing upright, in their tracks, the snow laid
on them like thick plaster. The man struggling with his load
felt the first stinging crystals and heard the first wind racing
around the bend in the cañon above him, and, when wet
flakes whipped at his back, he recognized the force of it and
tried to shrug the rope off so he could run for his cave, but
his flopping deerskins tangled in the loop and held it
around his waist. He worked it down to his knees before a
howl of wind knocked him flat on his back. All the air burst
out of his lungs, and the wind was a cold weight sitting on
his chest, and his feet were all tangled up in the rope tying
him to the bundle of posts.

He managed to twist over into a fetal position, drawing
his knees up and wrapping his arms around his face just so
he could breathe. The wind howled over him like a great
wolf gone mad. At first his instinct was to crawl away from
it, but the rope pulled at his legs. He bent around to get it
loose, but found he could not fight the rope and the wind at
the same time. The snow was coating him all over, sticking
even to his bare hands and face. And when the rope was finally loose, he no longer resembled a man or even a bear,
but only a white misshapen lump staggering before the
fierce wind, being thrown from one side of the cañon to the
other.

He squinted into the blizzard whipping snow in front of
his face, and once he thought he knew where he was and
that it was not far to the tunnel. But he had seen these blizzards before, had seen the cattle frozen standing in their
tracks, had known of men—and women—who went down

in the drifts and froze to death mere yards from their own doorways. He remembered a woman who had gone out in a blizzard like this to shut up her chicken coop fifty yards from her house, and they had found her two months later, when the snow melted, halfway between chicken coop and house. Her mouth was agape like someone suffocating.

A sudden blast knocked him to his knees, and he started to crawl, but it was like crawling inside a down-filled pillow, except for the freezing cold. His arms were sinking into the snow, up to the elbows. He saw that both of his hands were torn open and the flowing blood had frozen into ghastly patterns. Exhausted, sweating, freezing, bewildered, and lost, he finally fell over on his side and looked upward, waiting for the end to come.

It was then, when he had given up, that the ground blizzard began to let up and he could see a little farther. The wind was still howling and raging, but through streaks and gaps in the flying snow he thought he glimpsed the cañon rim. The blizzard was lifting up, rising on a fresh wind, leaving a layer of horrifying cold on the floor of the cañon. Protecting his eye with an upflung hand, he tried to see through the flying snow, tried to look up the cañon. Maybe the end of the storm would be coming down the cañon just like the other times. But panic seized his heart and froze his lungs until even the most shallow breath was a stabbing pain—the storm had taken the shape of a woman.

The wet, white bundle of rags and hides cried aloud when he saw her.

Her gown was a sweeping mass of white flung out from cañon rim to cañon rim and hundreds of feet into the snow-swirled air. Her flowing hair was white as well, and her long white arm raised a white hand with long white fingers reaching for him. Her eyes stared down at him, wide empty holes of blue in the snow-formed face, and her mouth gaped wide and there was nothing behind it but blue sky, yet it cried out and seemed to break his eardrums with wailing. Her outstretched arms had white mists flowing from them like cascades of foam, and now her wail turned into the same long, drawn-out rising howl as a wolf at bay, then changed to the tortured squealing of a pig feeling the butcher knife at its throat. The white woman's white mouth kept on opening and shutting in the air above him, the hands straining toward him. Mist flowing down from one arm looked like a ghostly quirt hanging there.

The ragged little bundle quivered in his heavy coating of soggy snow and threw his arms over his face. He screamed back at the banshee, and screamed and screamed until he heard the cañon throwing back his echo and the banshee and the wind were gone and he was alone in the softly falling snow.

Chapter Seven

THE KISS OF THE BANSHEE

Gwen Pendragon stood at the bedroom window watching the sunrise and brushing her hair. She loved to watch the spreading brightness of morning as it raced toward her, flooding across the prairie and over the little pine-speckled hills, striking and shining on the remaining drifts and pockets of snow. Each day she hoped to see small green shoots beginning to pop out on her fruit trees, or the first faint tinge of green spreading through the grass. After the hard winter, this early warmth of March made her even more anxious for summer.

"Art," she said, pointing with her hairbrush to a figure on the lawn, "who's that little boy down there?"

Art came to the window, buttoning his shirt. He looked down.

"Hmm," he said. "Looks like the McCarthy kid. Remember him? From the Christmas party? I wonder what he's doing down there. Looks like he's been standing there quite a while. Why didn't he knock on the door?"

"He's just a shy boy, Art. Don't you remember, at the party, how he stood against the wall and wouldn't talk to anybody? I finally got him to accept a plate of food, and he just sat in a corner and ate. He's the one who wouldn't open his Christmas package in front of everyone. Took it home with him still wrapped. I'll bet he came to see you about something, and he's too bashful to bother you. He'd probably stay out there all day, waiting, until someone came outside."

Art kissed Gwen's neck and let the fragrance of her loose hair flow over his senses. Sometimes he wanted to tell her she was too beautiful to stand at the window where any of the ranch hands might see her in her nightdress, and at other times he wanted the whole world to see her as he did.

"You'd better go down," she said reluctantly. "The poor boy is freezing out there."

Art growled, but agreed. He was starting to get other ideas, but he agreed.

The McCarthy boy sat stiffly on a kitchen chair, hat in lap, and smiled bashfully as Mary set a mug of warm milk and a plate of her fresh biscuits in front of him. Art took a biscuit and spread it with jam, indicating with a gesture of his table knife that the boy was to do the same. And he did.

"So you rode all the way here this morning," Art stated.

"I did."

"Your mother all right? And your brother?" Art asked.

"She is," the boy said between mouthfuls.

"OK," Art said.

Three biscuits later—two cups of coffee for Art—the reason for the boy's visit to the Keystone main ranch began to emerge. In fact, encouraged by Gwen's smile and Mary's milk and biscuits and jam, the boy became downright conversational.

"It's about the woman that's stayin' with us," the McCarthy boy finally volunteered.

"Who's that?"

"Missus Owen. From up in the mountains. She came a while after the Christmas party. There was that big storm and all, then, real late, there come a racket outside. Mother and me went out, and our dogs were barkin' somethin'

86

fierce at a team, standin' there at our gate. Didn't I think they were snow horses. Like snowmen? But they was real." He looked mournfully at the empty plate, and Mary quickly filled it again. "Sure I took 'em for white spooks."

"This lady said her name was Missus Owen?"

Gwen looked at Art in surprise.

"Yes, sir. Back last summer, a cowboy come through an' stayed the night in our barn. He wore a eye patch, and his name was Owen, too. Mother and this lady was talkin' about him, and the woman says he was her husband."

"What did she look like?" Gwen asked.

"I dunno," the McCarthy boy answered.

"Young? Older? Older than your mother, for instance?"

"I dunno. Not as old as mother by a long shot. Dark hair. Purty-lookin' lady. But not near so purty as. . . ." The boy looked at Gwen and stopped in mid-sentence. Suddenly embarrassed, he began picking biscuit crumbs off his plate with the end of his finger.

Art grinned. Few women were as "purty" as Gwen.

"And she came through that Christmas storm to your place?" Art said, "with a wagon?"

"No, sir. Bobsled, and a big 'un. Had two trunks of clothes on it and a couple of baskets. One had food in it. Right there, at first, she went on about bein' chased out by some gang of men, but by the time she got to our place, she was kinda out of her head. It's the cold, y'know, makes folks crazy."

"Does your mother need . . . ?"—Art knew better than to use the word help around these Irish grangers, proud as they were. "She need me to come talk t' this woman? Does your mother have enough room for a house guest?"

"Reckon that's why Mother sent me. She's a nice lady and helps out, and all, but she just don't belong there.

Least that's what we're thinkin'. Mother says she's more your kinda people."

"Oh," Art said. "Well. She's sure more than welcome here, and there's plenty of room. She could have one of the cabins, since we're down to just half a crew for the winter."

"Mother was reckonin'. . . ." The boy paused, eyeing the last biscuit on the plate.

"Better take it." Art grinned. "No sense leavin' just one."

"Mother was reckonin' maybe one of your people could come fetch Missus Owen. See, we don't wanna just tell her t' leave. It'd be different if she got an invite, see? And she's got them trunks and that team of hers is eatin' our winter hay, and I'm thinkin' there ain't enough snow 'tween here and our place for that big bobsled she come in on."

"So," Art said. "I guess a good idea would be for me to come along with a wagon and see if she'd like to come stay here."

"Mother'd be obliged," the McCarthy boy said. "I gotta be goin'."

"My father used to do this," Lady Fontana told Art. "Whenever I smell hot gunny sacks, it reminds me how he would wrap hot rocks and put them under the wagon seat to keep our feet warm. It's sad we sometimes lose all those childhood feelings."

She had the buffalo robe wrapped around her, capturing the heat from the rocks. She had to hold the burlap tightly between her shoes, because the stones shifted each time the wagon hit a bump. And there were plenty of bumps, since Art was avoiding snowdrifts on the road by going cross-country over the frozen ground. Her belongings were in the wagon bed, and her team was tied to the back.

"So that was your woman, the one who came this summer and lit into poor Kyle with his own quirt," Art said.

"Evidently it was. But I didn't know he was at the Keystone, nor did I know that she would go there. And she said some men were after her to kill her?"

"Tell you the truth, after it was over, I wasn't sure *what* she'd said. She just rode in, didn't even get off her horse. She called him all kinds of names, then hit him with his quirt, took it, and left. Said men were chasing her, or, at least, I think that's what she said. Anyway, *somebody* was after her. She wouldn't stay. Just rode off and vanished."

"Oh, dear. I think the men chasing her were the same ones who came to break the Great North diversion ditch and ruin us. Two or three of them were killed. Their leader flew into a rage and imprisoned me in my own house. They talked about hanging both of us!"

Art looked at her in disbelief. "Hanging? What outfit was this . . . that goes around lynching women?"

"They weren't with any ranch, if that's what you mean," Fontana replied. "The men seemed to belong to some kind of sect or religious group, something like that. You know that the Great North is . . . was . . . an irrigation project? Perhaps Kyle told you. Two years after Kyle was caught and taken away, these men arrived. A dozen of them. They announced they were building a settlement to the glory of God, and that the waters of God were needed. They diverted our main ditch in the mountains, and then dynamited all of the lower parts of it. Ruined. Years of labor, gone. They will tell you that's it's all legal, of course. I suppose I should have known it wouldn't last."

There was silence after that. Art was deep in thought, hardly aware of the bouncing of the wagon or the woman wrapped in the robes on the seat next to him. It would be awful, Art thought, the end of the world, to have all your work ruined like that. Art was tempted to say she was still rather young and attractive-looking and could start over, but it was still tragic that she should have to. Come spring, he might just take some men, maybe round up some hands from other ranches, and go see about this religious settlement. The more he thought about it, the madder he got. This sort of thing just couldn't be tolerated.

"I am glad Kyle found your ranch," Fontana said at last, breaking into his thoughts. "When Luned said four men had taken him away, we presumed . . . well, we did not think to see him alive again. He made many enemies, defending the Great North ditch."

"I guess he never told you that he used to work for me," Art said. "Kyle rode for the Keystone before he vanished up into the mountains. Another one of my Keystone riders, a young man named Will Jensen, went up there earlier. Some big gunslinger on a big horse stopped him and took everything he had. Broke Will's spirit. He started hittin' the bottle, and then drifted east. Well, Kyle couldn't stand the idea of it, so he went north into the mountains to find this gunman. When he didn't come back, we looked for him. Quite a few times. My riders put the word out to other ranches to watch for him, but it was like he vanished. A couple of years went by, and Will Jensen came back to us. He figured he knew where Kyle was, so he and I and two other riders made the trip up there. We found your big diversion ditch, and then this *hombre* began shootin' at us and it turned out to be Kyle. It was like he had gone crazy and out of his head, up there. But those four men who brought him back, that was us. Me, Pasque, Will Jensen, and the Pinto Kid."

"How ironic," she said. "After you took him away, I had workers searching for him. For a year or more. But you didn't know he was married to me?"

"We saw that ring he brought back, the one he braided onto his quirt. But he never talked about it, and nobody wanted to ask. He was pretty spooky for a long time and didn't really talk to anybody."

"Our settlement had no minister and no legal office or officials of any kind," Fontana explained. "The marriage was more or less my doing, a public announcement more than anything else. I'm sure he doesn't think of us as being legally married. I don't know why he would."

The day warmed up, as winter days will. Art gave her the history of the Keystone and its long struggle to get established, and how success had turned into a complicated business what with having five outlying ranches now and hundreds of employees, some of whom he had never even met. He talked about the growth of the cattle business, the enormous roundups when all the neighboring ranches sent hands to sweep the whole territory and sort out the brands. How it took weeks.

"After the big roundup," he told her, "me and the other ranchers, around here, end up without much to do and a lot of men on our hands. I'm thinking we ought to take some, maybe sixty to a hundred men, and go back up in the mountains and get your place back. With us backin' you, you ought to be able to straighten it out pretty good. Oh, and I tell you what . . . if the weather stays like this, I can send a couple of men out to look for Kyle. I'll have 'em look for your friend, too. What'd you call her?"

"Luned. I have no idea where you would look. She is such a strange young woman. But as for going back and having men risk their lives over the Great North project, no.

No, it's all over. Even if we could restore the ditch and make the water flow again, something would be lost. Crannog was the source of something and has been spoiled, ruined, violated. Whatever was there, the spirit of it came away with me, is in me. Someday. . . ."

The Keystone house came into view, together with the dozens of buildings and corrals of the main ranch. The horses caught the smell of warm hay and fresh water and stepped up their pace, and the wagon went jangling down the hill. For the horses it would be a good rubdown and freedom to roll in the sun. For the two chilly people on the wagon seat, it meant hot drinks and freshly baked pie beside the glowing kitchen stove.

Far away across many miles of prairie, the shaggy figure huddled in his stinking hides, too frozen to sleep. His teeth chattered, and he could not stop his mind from seeing the nightmare banshee. His barricade across the tunnel left the cave dark except for the glow of burning coals. He kept a few embers alive so there would be a way to light a grease torch when he needed to check on his chambers and tunnels. The smoke hung in the cave, eventually drifting up the coyote hole, but it didn't concern him. His eye was red and puffy, he coughed frequently, and a steady stream of mucus ran down into his mustache and beard, but he was indifferent to it.

Sometimes a fresh draft of air would find its way through the log barricade, sending his slumbering consciousness into a higher level of thought. When such a gust came, he would sit upright with his arms around his knees and stare through the gloom at the barricade, his breath almost suspended, waiting for the banshee to follow. Sometimes he heard it outside his cave, shrieking and howling for him.

The rest of the time was merely a long cycle of sleeping and eating and poking sticks into the coals.

Then one day a different kind of wind gust came into his reeking burrow, a quiet puff that stirred the air with news of spring. He lifted his head and sniffed, sensing that this new wind would not be followed by a howling white blizzard. There was a bit of damp earth in this new smell, and even some scent of green grass.

He stared at the tiny chink of light coming between the logs and wondered if anyone would come, now that the winter had broken. He thought of reasons why someone might come. Maybe somebody had spotted his smoke during the winter and would come to investigate. Maybe the homesteader would come back. Maybe it would be somebody looking for a place to dig another burrow. Such a person would find his burrow with its caves and tunnels well worth seeing. At times he almost wished some other cave dweller would crawl inside to appreciate the work that had gone into it, the ingenuity of his storage niches and his defenses. But the stranger might then want it and would not tell anyone else how to get in, but would scheme and plot to take over this roomy burrow rather than build his own.

If someone came, he muttered to himself, he would have to lure him inside and let him look around and exclaim over it all. He had his gun. He had wiped it with the grease and tried to keep it clean, but when he handled it in the dark, his fingers felt the grit on the metal. One day a deer had come grazing down the cañon, and, when Kyle saw it, he went and got the gun, but he snapped the hammer on three cartridges and none of them fired. He figured the damp had got to all his ammunition. But if an intruder came, he could seize up a firewood club or his old knife and kill him. He could then dig out a place to bury him in one of the blind tunnels, and no one would be the wiser.

No. What did he fear so much? What fear would make him kill another man? Fear of being discovered? Of never seeing his cave again? Besides that, a corpse buried in his cave would desecrate it. No, he thought, the thing to do is to go to the surface and greet anyone looking for caves and burrows, and then simply smile and tell him there are none here. Nothing to gain by staying here. Go away.

But what if . . . what if someone came who was not a threat? What if someone came who simply wanted to be with him? But even such a person would want to eat from his caches of tough dry meat and shriveled berries and roots. Such a person would need more fire, more light. Such a person would double the risk, with two people, instead of one, coming and going. Two people, though . . . he thought of the way the wolves and coyotes ran with their mates, a synchronized team of perfect movement, more like one animal in two bodies. Two people . . . could hunt together. One to watch the burrow while the other slept.

But, so far, he had been safe, and had enough to eat and enough fuel. Whether there were smells of spring in the air or not, he saw no need for another person. He scratched himself thoughtfully and rolled again to his side and went back to sleep.

In a few days he cautiously took down half the logs and let the fresh air rush in. A few days after that, he ventured to the mouth of the tunnel, then outside, then stood on the cañon floor. All was quiet. The sun had some warmth to it. He could not see the horizon, but he figured the whole sky was as clear blue as the strip he could see over the cañon. Small green shoots of grass were everywhere, and he had a hunger for fresh meat.

He returned to the cave and found the gun, but there was a film of rust all over it, and it was all he could do to get the hammer cocked or the cylinder to turn. The bullets, too, showed the effect of lying on a damp ledge. The brass had turned green, and he didn't think the powder would be any good. But he checked the six cartridges in the cylinder, anyway, and shoved the gun into what remained of his belt. He reached up into a long shelf above the tunnel entrance and took down his primitive spear, a thick straight shaft on which he had whittled a sharp point.

It felt good to be crawling up through the coyote hole, especially knowing that there would be no fierce white wind waiting for him to emerge in the rocks. He shifted the stone slab he used to seal up the opening and stood looking out over the prairie. A slight greenish tinge was upon the sage and yucca. Blue sky vaulted over the whole world from horizon to horizon. There should have been a gentle breeze, but there was not; there should have been small springtime calls of the prairie birds and cries from circling hawks, but there was not.

He slouched so quietly and still against the cedar tree on the rocky outcrop that anyone passing by would have taken him for a tree stump or small boulder. He was listening for the coyotes. Somewhere out there, they were hunting. Rabbit, maybe, or deer. He licked his lips. A haunch of fresh venison, popping and sizzling in a bed of coals. He waited. He listened. There would be yelping from the animals, and they would have meat.

Instead of the cry of the pack, he heard a faint sound of something moving in the brush. Something chewing, something moving. Something grazing. Very, very slowly he turned and scanned the sage. All was silent and still as death except for the small foot movements of something moving. He studied the terrain methodically, letting his gaze stay on one patch of sagebrush or one rise of sandy earth for a long time, memorizing all the details, before moving to the next. And then he saw it. Between his rock outcrop and the edge of the cañon, almost hidden in the high brush, was a yearling steer. Or young cow, he couldn't tell. But it wasn't a deer or an antelope. It was the color of a range steer, but small. A stray, a maverick.

He took several minutes to get down on his knees, very gradually sinking down as if melting into the ground. Meanwhile, he planned his route, scheming each movement that would get him from where he was to where it was. It would be moving, too, as it grazed the young shoots of grass. He visualized himself crawling to a yucca, bellying down through a shallow depression, then hiding behind a clump of sage. He'd be close enough to attack with his spear. He wouldn't take a chance on the gun, since it might not go off.

Crawling forward gradually, controlling his breathing, picturing exactly how he would plunge the spear into the animal right behind the shoulder, he had a sudden shuddering memory of guarding the ditch and sneaking up on human intruders. Now once more he felt ice in his blood and death in his eye. Stalking filled his head with blood and excitement, but his body remained calm and controlled. His hands felt icy cold while his forehead flushed with heat. He stopped and listened.

The yearling had either smelled him or had sensed him. It was also standing stockstill, suspicious, muscles tensed. Then it decided to move away. He heard its footsteps turning in the other direction, and he charged from the sagebrush, a man-size apparition of rags and hides and tatters and hair, waving a long stick. The animal gave out one

96

high-pitched bellow of terror, lowered its head, and lashed out with its hind legs at the thing coming at it, made a feint to the right and dodged back to the left, plowed through a sage thicket, throwing broken twigs and dirt up in a cloud as it went, then ran through a thick yucca where the green bayonets stabbed at its belly. It went straight over the edge of the cañon.

The stalker shambled to the edge. The yearling had fallen more than twenty feet and broken its neck, crashing to the cañon floor a few yards from the tunnel opening. It lay there perfectly still, stretched out as if ready for butchering. A little breeze rose and flicked at the man's rags and hair. He sniffed it. He looked down at his meat, lying there. He looked into the breeze and it felt cold on his face and he could see the storm coming, a mound of gray sky against the blue growing with incredible speed, coming down the cañon. It seemed to have risen up out of the sage, out of nowhere, and seemed bent on nothing except catching him.

Now it was his turn to run for his life. He plunged down the coyote hole without replacing the flat rock over it; he left his spear somewhere in the tunnel because it was awkward; he bumped into corners and protruding roots in the darkness as he scrambled downward and downward to reach his cave, his burrow. When he got there, he had a cut over his eye and blood ran from his filthy hands. He worked at the logs, managing to get the first one into place, but jamming the second one so that it wouldn't drop into position. Then he thought of that fresh meat out there.

He clambered over the logs, yelling defiance as he rushed through his tunnel and outside into a weird light that left no shadows. Now the sudden snow was hurling itself at him in great globs, and coming so fast and so thick that he could not see. Even when he sheltered his eye against the driving slaps of the thick wet snow, he could not see. He was stumbling around like a blind man, torn between wanting the meat and fearing he could not find his tunnel again. He looked backward, and all was white and everything invisible and the wind clawed at his face. He looked forward and could only try to imagine where the dead yearling might be, or where he was himself.

And the howling once more arose in the cañon.

Low at first, like a far-off drawn-out booming, it came curling up over him as it had done before. It became a shrill screeching like an iron bar scraping stone, increasing until his ears must surely be bleeding.

Then came the inhuman howling.

The swirling snow whipped up and away and left gaps of blue against which there was again the figure of a flying woman, mouth agape, eyes empty, her white cloak spread out far above him. She leaned down toward the cañon, crying at him. He took a step or two back in fear and fell over the still-warm body of the yearling cow. This time there was not enough snow in the storm to bury and smother him, but enough to leave him soaking wet. Now the wind went to work to freeze him and the cow carcass into one frigid mass. But worse than the freezing wind was the screaming and screaming, coming from the gaping face that hovered over the cañon.

He drew the gun from his rags. His shivering fingers cocked it and aimed at the specter. There was only the *thud* of the rusted hammer as it came down on a worthless cartridge. Staring up into the storm, he thought the banshee's face was coming down at him. He closed his eye against it, but the icy mouth clamped over his own lips, and he thought he was drowning just before he passed out.

Gwen Pendragon and Fontana Owen took advantage of the spring weather to ride the fields and pastures of the home ranch. Gwen laughed at newborn calves, leaping and running, but Fontana was more apt to say that it was sad the animals would have only one or two years to live. They stopped to admire the new colts as they ran beside the mares or stood, legs splayed far apart, trying to graze on the new grass. Fontana spoke pragmatically about how they would be broken to become work horses.

In the evenings the ladies sat by the fireplace while Art talked about the hard winter and his plans to re-stock the range. Sometimes Link or one of the other foremen would stop in. One evening, Link and Art and Gwen heard the story of Fontana's escape from Crannog, her home in the faraway mountains.

"These men, the ones I told you about, left us alone most of the winter. But when the snow began to melt and they could force a trail through the drifts and up over the pass, they came frequently. Always the same five or six, led by an angry man who had a full beard down to his stomach. Sometimes they would take over one of my worker's homes, forcing the family to take shelter with neighbors. They would ride around like they were surveying the place, taking stock of what they were going to have, once the snow was all gone.

"Luned left after . . . well, two of them were killed, and another, who was with them, blamed her for it. They couldn't blame me, of course. And Luned comes and goes like air. No one controls her. Not me, not anyone. That fact provided their leader with an opportunity to lecture me and torment me.

"Some of my workers began to side with them. From my

window I watched them talking to the bearded pirate who ran things, nodding their heads in agreement with whatever he was saying. He never dared to enter my house, but he would ride up to the porch and call for me to come out. And if I did, he would preach scripture at me, all about how women must be obedient and subservient, and then he would ride off.

"My chance finally came when we had a hard freeze late in the winter, in late February or early March. Maybe you had the same thing here. There was a long storm, then a bad freeze. I still had one man I could trust, my hostler. He came and told me I should take the bobsled and team and escape by driving down the ditch to the foothills, and then turn south. He said no horsemen would be able to get through the pass, and I would have a week's head start on them.

"He turned out to be right. I started before first light one morning, taking only a couple of trunks of clothes, a food hamper, and all the blankets and buggy robes I could manage to wrap around me. Fortunately, once the hostler got the team into the ditch for me, all I needed to do was encourage them to keep moving. There was no way for them to get out, and the layer of snow on the ice was perfect for the sled runners.

"Anyway, after two very, very cold nights in the open and several more nights with settlers, I discovered Missus McCarthy's place. Imagine how surprised I was when she told me Mister Owen had been there earlier."

"Things like that happen quite a lot out here." Link smiled. "I suppose it's because there are so few people. Almost all the roads lead to the same places. I remember . . . you'd remember this, Art . . . an Englishman came to see about investing money in cattle, and one day he happened to mention a cousin living out West. Darned if this cousin didn't own a store right there in town."

The meeting between Fontana Owen and the Pendragons was a fortunate one. Art struggled daily with bookkeeping chores that seemed to get more complicated every time he hired a new man or acquired a few more cattle or another bit of range. Suddenly along came this woman who enjoyed that kind of work. So, in return for doing Art's "desk drudgery," Fontana was given a safe, warm place to live. He was also glad to pay her a salary. Any amount of money was worth it, if he could get away from the desk and out into the open air again.

The bad winter they had been through made summer all the more busy. Men had to be sent to scour hundreds of square miles of range and scout hundreds of draws and valleys for whatever remained of the winter herds of cattle. Others had to be sent for replacement stock. Each animal needed attention, whether it was branding, earmarking, vaccination, dehorning, or castration. Each one had to be accounted for, usually by one of the *segundos* sitting on his horse, knee cocked around the saddle horn, his forehead wrinkled as he studiously used a stubby pencil to make entries in his small notebook.

The word went out all over the range, from ranch to ranch, for men to watch for Kyle Owen, tall and slim and with a patch over one eye, and for a woman called Luned, slim and small and pale. Cowboys took the search seriously, to the point of going out of their way to inquire at granger soddies or to ask soldier patrols about the missing man and woman.

Ironically it was Will Jensen who came nearest to the cañon with the secret burrow. He had been across the border, looking for men to hire, and he decided to return to

101

the ranch by way of the old Texas Cattle Trail and the Deadwood Stage Road. Will figured he had the time and Art might like to know how things looked out in that neck of the woods.

On the stage road Will overtook a double rig, two heavy freight wagons loaded with bales of wool. They were coupled together and pulled by a ten-horse string team. The driver and his swamper were a little nervous at first, having a gun-toting cowboy ride up alongside their wagon. Cowboys and sheep didn't mix too well. But Will only asked about Kyle and Luned.

"Nope. Ain't seen a good-lookin' woman in weeks," the driver said. "Other fella was a cowboy, y' say."

"That's right," Will answered. "A one-eyed man. Maybe you saw him somewhere."

"Nuthin' such as thet," the swamper said. "Seen a three-legged coyote along here, last trip. Seen an Injun what has two fingers missin'."

"Say," the driver said to the swamper, "don't you recollect when we stopped alongside the stagecoach at thet waterhole las' month? Passengers was sayin' they'd seen a old Injun or somethin' skulkin' in the sagebrush out yonder, somewheres. All dressed in animal skins."

"Well," Will said, "that wouldn't be our man. But if y' happen to hear anything, leave word anywhere. Keystone Ranch. Just leave word for the Keystone at a stage station. It'll get to us, sooner or later."

Will touched his quirt to his horse and rode on, leaving the two wagons and their teams plodding along. Within the sound of a pistol shot, a hunched figure in rags squatted on his look-out rock, gnawing away at a strip of jerked beef.

Chapter Eight

THE BLACK COATS

Late spring brought an abundance of color, even to the sage flats. The mustard color of blooming rabbitbrush and snakeweed was everywhere, and every rise of ground had a sprinkling of blue larkspur or golden banner, pale lavender loco or stark white sego lilies. Even the horsenettle and bindweed and cacti were covered in blossoms. The grass, encouraged by March snowstorms and April rains, stretched tough green stems toward the sky.

Art Pendragon rode more often and farther than he had done in several years. Partly it was to survey the range and estimate the risk of re-stocking it with cattle. The grass looked good enough that he might be able to make up for the devastating winter. But wherever he rode, he was also looking for Kyle. Sometimes he waited by the stage road to talk with the drivers and teamsters passing by. He took a bedroll and a sack of food and went into Dakota, to the mining settlements, to see if Kyle had been there. It was like the old days when he used to make long rides, alone or with a couple of good men, buying stock at remote settlements and latchstring ranches.

Link often went with him. Sometimes they came across folks who needed them. Once it was a friend, a rancher from up in the Frenchman Creek flats, hobbling along through the hills. His horse had given out and his feet were about to, and he was mighty glad when the two riders showed up. Another time they helped three lost immigrant wagons get on the right trail again. The immigrants spoke of crossing a railroad right-of-way, two days since, and seeing gangs of men laying rails, and one had an eye patch.

A day and a half later, Art and Link caught up with the construction crew. There was a one-eyed man, all right, but he weighed around two hundred and fifty pounds and was bald as an egg. They spent the night with the crew, careful to sleep on their wallets and guns, and they didn't ask how the big man had lost his eye.

The wild-goose chase took them east into country neither of them had seen before. Flat and empty it was, with little water. Arroyos and draws and cañons cut through it in all directions so that they often had to ride for hours just to find a way to cross over. On the third night, along toward dusk, they saw a campfire against a low butte and headed for it. It was a camp of a half-dozen crude lodges made of Army tarps wrapped around crooked poles.

The two riders sat at a polite distance. After the Indians were reasonably sure they were alone and not part of a military detachment, one came out on his pony and raised his hand. Art and Link rode forward.

"Howdy," Art said.

"Howdy," the young Indian mimicked.

"Speak English?" Art said.

"Yes," the Indian said. He studied Art's face carefully, then Link's.

"Hunting?"

"Yes."

"We hunt a man," Art said. "We do not know where to find him."

"Oh."

Art cupped one hand over his eye, like a patch. "Man with one eye. One eye covered, like this. Tall. Cowboy."

The Indian gestured for the two Keystone men to follow him, and then turned and rode back to the camp. Link held the horses while Art went to talk to the leader. He figured them to be Arapahos, from the way they had their hair tied up, but both the English-speaking young man and the older man, who was the leader, kept saying "Cheyenne." Of course, it was legal for the Cheyennes to be hunting and wandering around out in this area. The Arapahos were supposed to stay on the reservation.

A woman brought water for them, and the three began to speak. The older man was quite sympathetic. He, too, had lost warriors in the same manner. They had gone out to hunt and had never returned or been heard of again. Perhaps Art should look where the *wasichus* make the iron road. Art replied that he had looked there. Perhaps this cowboy is to be found in the fort where the bluecoats live.

"Fort Laramie?" Art asked.

"Kearney," the young man volunteered. "Might be."

"Perhaps," Art said.

The older man then began speaking rapidly, his forehead wrinkling in serious thought. When he had finished, the younger Indian turned to Art again.

"He is afraid the man-bear has eaten your cowboy."

"Man-bear? What man-bear?"

The young man pointed southwest. He himself had not seen this thing, but the older man and another elder had seen it. A place not far from the stagecoach road. A place of rocks near a cañon. They had seen what they thought was a very big coyote, sunning itself, and, when they had approached it, they had been surprised to see it jump up on its hind legs and roar at them. They knew it was a man-bear, part man and part bear, and would eat them. When they turned to look back, they saw it crawl into the rocks and vanish. They went away from that place and would not go back. Probably a spirit bear that has eaten so many men, he has become half man.

"Our friend carried guns," Art said solemnly. "He is a very good shot. Surely he could kill such an animal."

"It might be so," the Indian said. "We do not know if this man-bear is still alive or not."

The older man looked thoughtful at hearing this, and then offered another idea.

"Maybe he is with the black coats," the young man said.

"Who are the black coats? We don't know where they are."

The young Indian translated this question to his elder, who cackled a little laugh and said something.

"He says the *wasichus* say they live a long time here but lose the other *wasichus*. He says it is because there are too many of you. The black coats came from the place of the Shoshonis, two seasons ago. They make houses of dirt,"— the young man's hands performed as if making adobe bricks, and he went on. "They plow land, much land. They make water come to them."

"Sounds like a farming settlement of some kind. Why black coats?"

"All wear black coats. Their women wear"—he made motions as if putting on a bonnet.

"Could be Mormons," Link said.

"Could be anybody," Art said. "Could be those same ones that ran Fontana off her place."

The young man pointed in the general direction of the settlement of black coats, and Art and Link rode off. The Indians were not sorry to see them go, and Art and Link were more comfortable once they were out of sight of the camp.

"Arapahos, I figure," Art said, "off the reservation."

"Yeah," Link agreed. "Let's get across this next arroyo before we make camp."

The man in the cave felt the warmth of spring and the heat of June and lost some of his fear. Like the owl or the fox he went hunting in the dark early hours of morning, sometimes returning to the cave with rabbits or prairie chickens. As the grass grew tall, he pulled armloads of it and stacked it in niches and tunnels to dry for bedding. He watched the fruit ripen, the wild plum and chokecherry, the prairie turnips. He followed the coyote pack and learned where the wolf pair hunted, and took more than one deer away from them.

As June turned to July and then to August, the shaggy figure spent the day inside the cool tunnels and went out after sunset. He gathered wood from both sides of the cañon, having found a steep animal trail leading up the other side. Always he went on digging, widening the tunnels, deepening the storage niches, planning a second room. This room would be secret, impossible for intruders to find; for many hours he sat cross-legged on the floor of the cave, chewing strips of meat, figuring how to hide a room.

The solution did not satisfy him, but it was all he could do. He climbed up onto the slope of the mesa and searched out a big flat slab of rock. He could not lift it, but he could tip it on edge and roll it, a few feet at a time. In this manner he got it to the edge and pushed it over. He rolled it across the cañon floor, across the small creek, and up to his tunnel. When he got it inside and leaned it against the wall, he dusted off his hands with satisfaction.

With his one eye, he squinted around in the gloom for

watchers, and began to dig. This would be the best tunnel yet. Nothing, man or animal, would be able to drag him from this final hiding place. He worked slowly, relishing the idea of it. The project would take a long, long time. The tunnel would go down into the floor of the cave, against the wall. It would be big enough for his body. When it was deep enough, he planned to tunnel under the cave wall and dig out another room on the other side. The stone would cover the hole, and, with firewood stacked on it, no one would suspect where it was.

The summer also yielded more beef. The coyote pack brought down a stray calf, and he claimed his share. Days later the animals chased another yearling near the rock out-crop where he lay sunning himself. He hunched down, hiding himself in the rocks, waiting for the right moment. He jumped up waving his rags and hides and croaking in his broken voice. The pack yelped and sprinted for the sage, forgetting their prey. The man-bear ran flapping and croaking until the panic-stricken animal plunged over the edge. This fall crippled it but did not kill it.

He cracked its skull with a rock and chuckled as he began to saw away at the body with his knife. Another good hide for his cave floor. Good bones to smash open and boil. Enough jerky to last a long time.

By October he was ready for winter. Each day he slouched outside and stood in the cañon looking north and sniffing the air for the banshee wind. Once his new hiding room was finished he would have no need to go out, not to get meat, not to get logs for a barricade. She would come howling at his door but would not find him.

He slept more and more. He ate less. During the times of waking, he crawled about in his tunnels, sometimes finding one he had forgotten in which the light of his grease torch no longer showed handprints or knee prints in the fine dust, as if he had never been there before. Some of these forgotten tunnels had caches of firewood and dried meat. He sometimes went into the coyote den to sleep because the surroundings felt and smelled differently. He used the coyote tunnel to go up onto the surface, but no longer followed the pack to steal food. He had enough food. He did not like the wind in the juniper tree, so he did not stay there to watch for intruders.

The new shaft did not go well. He managed to dig down far enough to conceal his body, if he bent his knees and hunkered down. He did not experiment with the stone lid. He began a tunnel from this shallow shaft, starting back under the wall of the main cave. It was slow work, hauling dirt outside and sluicing it into the creek. At the first snow he would have to find other ways to conceal the dirt. At the first snow, she would be back.

He had forgotten about water. He would have to go outside for it, sometimes. He would have to be quick and careful.

One afternoon he was scraping dirt out of the new hole when he heard a whistle. He stopped. He groped in his rags and brought out a chunk of jerky, which he chewed thoughtfully as he listened. What could it be? It was as if a kettle were boiling on a stove inside the cave wall. As he listened, the sound rose and fell like the sound of breathing. He hoisted himself out of the hole and scurried to the first tunnel. He crawled up it and lay still and listened, the chunk of meat forgotten in his mouth. First, silence. Then the whistling seemed louder, still rising and falling. He did not want to be trapped, so he scrambled back into the main cave and turned this way and that. There was no sound except the sound of the breeze outside the tunnel. He got down on his knees and crawled up the coyote tunnel to listen. It began again, a high-pitched monotone drone like a boy whistling through his teeth. Even with his hands over his ears, he heard the sound.

Back in the cave he tried to make sense of it. Maybe air was coming into the burrow through holes left by gophers or burrowing insects. He took a torch and soon found such a place in one of the tunnels, a small hole left by a gopher. He packed it with dirt, pounding it with his hand, shoving more dirt in, packing it into the hole with a stick, frantic to stop the whistling. He went through each tunnel, looking at the walls, jamming dirt into any hole he found, even tiny holes such as ants might leave.

But the whistling went on. And on. Fatigued from scrambling through tunnels, he finally fell asleep in the main cave, and his dreams were haunted by the noise. He woke to it and forgot to eat, and went off again in search of the source. Sometimes he believed it was an invisible creature playing tricks on him. Sometimes it seemed to be many small creatures whistling in unison to drive him out. He sat on the floor next to his small smudge of a fire and tried to think.

Maybe it was water making the noise. Water could be running behind his walls and making a sound like escaping air. But surely water would sound differently, gurgling or bubbling. Or it was she, putting her frozen white mouth over the coyote tunnel and blowing her chill breath at him. He hurried to block the opening with rocks. He went back to the cave entrance and lugged the barricade logs into place. When he sat, exhausted, with his back against it, the whistling noise went on rising and falling.

Day after day it kept up. When he squinted through the chinks, he saw that the dim light coming in the tunnel had a different glow to it, and he knew what it meant: snow. Only the snow made that kind of light. He huddled in his nest of dry grass and slept. He woke and chewed jerky, put bits of wood on the smoldering fire, slept again. He dreamed of a beast coming toward him through the earth, tunneling toward his burrow, and the beast looked like him. It was shaggy and had one eye, and the eye had a wild, burning stare. Sometimes he dreamed of a dozen animals, a pack whistling to each other while digging tunnels toward him. He woke up trembling and freezing and built up the fire until it crackled and blazed, not caring whether anyone saw the smoke coming from the coyote tunnel. At least, when the fire was crackling, he couldn't hear the whistling.

It was better to sleep, even with the dreams, but he could not stay asleep all the time. When he was awake, he tried to make sense of the sound. He tried whistling himself, in all the ways he could remember. He whistled through his teeth, with two filthy fingers between his cracked lips. He tried it with his mouth open and through his cupped palms, but he could not make the sound he heard coming through his walls.

He thought the sound might be an animal digging in the earth beyond his burrow, but he didn't know how. He scraped the wall with the shovel and with his long broken nails, but could not make the sound.

He tried to escape from it. He crawled into every tunnel, and the sound came with him. He crawled to the stones blocking the coyote tunnel, and listened and did not hear the sound coming from outside, but he could feel the freezing air and knew that death was waiting up there for him.

Once he went into a short tunnel to retrieve firewood

and food, and he heard it distinctly just on the other side of the tunnel wall; with a sly, crafty look he backed quietly down into the main cave for his shovel. It was still coming. He clawed at the wall, like a small rodent would, to lure the thing toward the tunnel. And then, just as he imagined it was about to break through, he crawled backward and stabbed furiously at the roof to collapse it and trap the thing inside. He put his ear to the obstruction, and the sound had ceased.

It returned in his dreams. He found it would not follow him out into the cañon when he went out for snow to melt for water, but he did not dare stay out there. One calm day, when it looked safe to go out, the glare of the sun on the crusted snow blinded him and sent him back into the comfortable gloom of the cave, his eye aching with excruciating pain. On another day, gray and overcast, he ventured out to see if he could fill his bucket at the stream, if it were not frozen. The snow was mushy underfoot. He managed to scoop up half a bucket of water where the ice had opened, but the warning wind came soughing down the cañon, and he saw the banshee face beginning to form on the gray mass of clouds to the north, so he limped and lurched back into his tunnel again.

He was in a trap. Not a hiding place, a trap. The thing outside waited to kill him, while the thing inside kept burrowing away at his walls. He could not do anything as long as it was there; he had not made a new tunnel or cache for weeks; he had forgotten to move his firewood piles from place to place, had not changed the grass in his bedding. He used to plan tunnels, elaborate tunnels leading up to the surface; he remembered a plan to make a duplicate burrow farther down the cañon, just in case.

But now he had to stay in his hole and keep quiet, so he

could hear the whistling sound. He listened for it to break through the wall or come down one of the tunnels. He fell asleep, listening, a pile of rags and hides in the smoky gloom, curled up in a nest of old grass.

The last clear note of Fontana's song floated up into the log rafters to the applause of Gwen, who was seated at the piano, and Art, who was warming his backside at the fireplace.

"Beautiful!" Gwen exclaimed. "I can't tell you how wonderful it is to have you here! In years past, Art has been such a grumpy bear this time of year. Pacing around every evening, honestly! But I really think we have managed to keep his mind busy in the evenings."

"Oh, I love it, too," Fontana said, putting the sheet music on top of the piano. "It's no good to mope around all evening, staring into the fire or reading some gloomy novel."

"Now, hush! You don't know what a struggle I've had to get Art to read Tolstoy instead of those awful things by Augusta Evans he's always getting in the mail!"

Fontana smiled, wishing she could recall the name of some other author, some compromise between the silly and the gloomy. She would not presume to tell the Pendragons how to spend their evenings, but it did seem to her that Gwen might take up something practical, such as quilting or needlepoint. Art might be better employed with books other than novels. Music made the long dark evenings go faster, but she wished for some new instrument to learn, some new music.

"I see you have a BOOK OF MORMON," she said, noticing the volume on the mantle.

Art glanced at it.

"Left here by a young fellow trying to catch up with his family. They were heading to Utah to join up with the Brigham Young bunch."

"And are you going to convert?" Fontana asked.

"God, no! I like working for myself, not for some 'common good'. And one wife is plenty for me, thanks!"

"Just an intellectual interest, then? Perhaps we could read some of it and discuss different beliefs."

"Tell the truth, I've been wondering about these black coats those Indians told us about. I got a letter the other day from a friend with a ranch up that way. He's coming this month to talk about longhorns. And he mentioned a colony of Mormons building up a community near him. I thought maybe the book would tell me what they're all about."

Fontana's face became serious.

"I didn't want to say anything at the time . . . I am *so* grateful to you for taking me in, and I *do* hate to dwell on my problems . . . but I'm sure I know who your black coats are."

"You do?" Art said.

"I think so. This is second-hand information from a young couple that came looking for work at Crannog. They had been with the Mormons in Salt Lake, but they wanted to get married, and their parents were against it. The church sided with the parents, so the two young people took up with a splinter group. Something happened with that . . . I didn't understand what . . . and they ran away.

"At any rate, when a gang of men came to claim the Great North water, the young man instantly identified the leader as this break-away bishop.

"From what the young man said," Fontana continued, "their scheme is to bring water to some unclaimed sections along the foothills and build a Mormon city there. The leader is a fat, strange man, but has at least a hundred followers."

Art's friend arrived and confirmed Fontana's explanation. He and his neighbors had visited the new colony, where they found men and women industriously planting vegetables and fruit trees, even varieties that had never before grown that far north. They had an irrigation system, a big one. They manufactured adobe brick for their houses and a compound, and in the middle of it they had an adobe fort.

"Not quite the size of the ol' Fort Bridger, before crazy Jim blew it up," he laughed, "but you'd still think they was expectin' a war."

"Well," Art said, "that tallies with what the Arapahos told us about the dirt houses and the black coats and all. I reckon the next thing we need to figure out is. . . ."

" 'Cept that one woman," the friend interrupted.

"What?"

"That one woman. I been over there, oh, I dunno, half a dozen times to dicker for vegetables and such-like, and a couple of times I seen this woman in a white dress. Tell the truth, I think they're keepin' her prisoner or sumthin'."

Fontana went pale. With shaking hands, she very carefully returned her teacup to the saucer.

"What did she look like?"

"Oh, kinda pale. Young. Purty skinny, too. They keep her in that fort of theirs, but the gate's usually open, and I seen her walkin' around in there."

"Art!" Fontana said. "I think it's Luned! Do you suppose they caught her?"

"Luned?" the man asked.

"Yes. She is . . . my friend. Those men seized our irrigation project. She killed two of them and ran away, but they pursued her. She stopped here at the Keystone, then rode on without so much as dismounting."

Art went to his desk and shuffled papers until he found the roster of Keystone riders.

"We'd better go see," he said, counting names. "I figure we can mount at least a dozen riders. Let's see . . . Link, the Pinto Kid, Bob, Dick Elliot. I've got six men up on the Lucy Fork. They could come in."

"Not enough," the friend said.

"What?"

"Art, you're lookin' at maybe a hundred guns there. The only time they ain't fully armed is when they're workin' the fields. They got a fort, storage buildings full of food, plenty of water. . . . I don't think the U.S. Cavalry could blast 'em outta there."

"Which might be exactly what they're afraid of," Art said.

"Yep."

Fontana looked to Gwen, then back to Art.

"Whatever you do," she said, "for God's sake, let's not risk any lives. I couldn't bear it if anyone else died over this. Luned is very clever, and she may find a way to escape. But we have to be very, very careful. Please, please, don't put anyone in danger."

"Well. . . ."

"Art," Gwen said, "surely they aren't harming her, if she's walking about. I'm for waiting until you can contact the other ranchers, possibly the Army. I know you and Link would love to go riding in with guns blazing to rescue the woman, even though she was the one who drove Kyle away from here, but we just have to wait."

Art looked at his wife. She was right. The Keystone was seriously outgunned. He would have to take the time to talk to the other ranchers and get in touch with Fort Laramie. And he needed more information before going all that distance with a couple of dozen men and all the supplies they would need.

"The ladies are right," he said to his friend. "Tell you what . . . when you get back, you and your neighbors sort of carefully see what you can find out, then telegraph me. We gotta know for sure who she is, and whether she's being kept there like a prisoner. Damn, I need a drink! Let's find one, and talk about those longhorns. The thing I was thinkin' is that we can breed 'em with red Herefords. . . ."

Chapter Nine

RIDDLE AND RENEWAL

The creature in the dark burrow lay by the smoldering fire, knees drawn up, head cradled in folded arms. From time to time it rocked back and forth, moaning. Most of his days passed in the same kind of stupefied hibernation; he roused himself sluggishly only when he needed a mouthful of dried meat or had to put a few sticks of wood on the little fire. If there was no breeze outside, it meant there was no draft through the coyote tunnel and the smoke hung in the cave so thick that he could breathe only by keeping his face next to the floor. But this did not bother him, after a time. He would only curl up there or in his grass nest and fold his arms over his ears in an effort to silence the whistling noise.

One day there was a new brightness in the cañon tunnel. Bright light, sunlight, penetrated almost to the log barricade, and he could see it through the chinks. At first he only sat there and chewed a piece of meat and looked at the log wall and contemplated it. It was not as if he were reasoning it out, or even wondering at it. He just sat and looked. Hours went by, and the brightness faded as the sun passed over the cañon and left the western precipice in shadow once again, and night came, and the brightness came back in the morning.

Again he sat and stared, eating. Then he roused himself and shambled toward the barricade and removed the logs. He wiped the back of a hand across his eye and went out into the cañon. He found the air warm and the sun brilliant.

It hurt to look at it. Some instinct told him it was not yet spring, yet neither was it the dead of winter. He lurched and shambled to the creek and found a thin line of open water. As he hunched down to drink, a little breeze ruffled and tugged at his rags and shaggy hair, but he did not seem to notice. He suddenly remembered the horse. A horse can make a kind of whistle noise, sometimes, in rutting season. Maybe that was the whistling noise he was always hearing. It hurt his feet to walk in the old boots, broken open and tied up with strips of stiff deer skin, but he walked down the cañon, looking into side cañons, behind brush and trees for sign of the horse. He found none, of course—the animal had long since strayed away to fall victim to some predator. But he had not thought of the horse for a very, very long time, and now the idea of it would not leave his mind.

The breeze behind him became chill.

He found tracks of either a cougar or a wolf. He couldn't tell. Something had come to drink at the stream. The tracks were just visible enough to follow, at least for a few hundred yards. They might lead him to a fresh kill, so he licked at his cracked lips and followed them as far as he could. If he went far enough, he might find the horse.

The breeze struck at his legs and reached around his head to tangle his long hair into his beard, so he crouched over and kept following the tracks. When they came to solid rock and vanished, he stood and puzzled over it for a moment. His mind gradually drew back from the idea of the tracks, passed over the idea of the horse, and came to realize that he was in a cold wind. He drew his hides and rags about him and turned to look into it, his one eye glowering through the greasy strands of wind-blown hair. Leaden clouds made a curtain on the northern horizon and flowed down into the cañon. Higher, touched by sunshine without warmth, fierce white clouds were tangling and billowing into the gray.

He ran. It was a stumbling, painful, pitifully slow and awkward running, but he ran.

The winter storm clouds lined themselves up with the cañon and drove forward, the leading edge in the shape of a woman's head and shoulders. She leaned forward out of the cloud bank and waited for him. He stumbled against rocks and slipped on a patch of ice. His chest hurt. His lungs burned. He threw one arm across his face to block out the sight of the storm and kept going. He did not know how far down the cañon he had gone in search of the long-vanished horse or the possibility of a recent kill, but he did know that his chances of making it back to the tunnel were not good.

She waited to strike at him until he came lurching around the last corner of the cañon and could see the mound of earth hiding his tunnel. Up until then he had been running into a chilling wind, but, as he sighted the earth mound, he felt himself twisted and flung flat to the ground by a blast of air colder than the grave. He wanted to draw up his knees and huddle against it, but to do so would be suicide. He struggled to his feet and went forward again. This time she shrieked at him. She screamed into his face and ripped him with flying ice crystals. But he went on, bent into it, protecting his face as best he could.

He was almost at the mound. She howled and seemed to relent for a moment, then smashed him sideways to send him sprawling against a boulder. He clung to it for his life, no longer able to protect his face with one arm. When he looked up into the blizzard, he was a supplicant looking into the axe-man's hooded face. But the face of the banshee wore no hood, only a cloak of graying white that the fierce winds frayed out all around her. Her enormous eyes were an icy blue. Her mouth was a horrid cavern of darkness, shrieking down at him. The wind circled and circled, whipping him with ice.

Dimly his mind dredged up a story of long ago, a piece of folklore. If a grizzly got a man in its jaws, they said, the man should play 'possum, pretend to be dead, and the grizzly would let go.

The man let go of the rock and dropped face down and lay still.

The banshee raged on, and then paused to lift her face to the cañon rim. The wind driving the snow into his flesh seemed to pause, too. The man gathered his strength under him and jerked to his feet. He threw himself forward in a run that was more of a series of limps, and plunged into the darkness of his tunnel. There he tripped and smashed full length on the tunnel floor but went on clawing his way forward into the cave. He put up his barricade, smashing a frozen finger in the process, then dumped a pile of wood on the smoldering fire pit and lay down and tried to curl himself around it.

He wept in defeat.

At least a month went by, or so it seemed to the trapped creature, but he did not venture outside again. He would take down the barricade and walk through the tunnel to peer out to see new green grass and feel the welcome warmth, but he would not go past the mouth of the tunnel. He sometimes went up to sleep in the coyote den where he would listen at the coyote tunnel for any sounds of anything moving up on the cañon rim. He thought he might even welcome the sight of dust rising on the faraway stage road, or the sounds of horsemen riding near his burrow.

He was in the coyote den, half asleep, when she found

her way in and came for him. He sensed the sudden new movement of air and shivered against it, and then his nostrils twitched at the smell of wood smoke, heavier than usual. He stirred and shifted, putting his head into the tunnel leading back into the cave, and he heard a sound as if some animal was in his woodpile tossing the sticks and branches all about. He mumbled angrily as he went down the tunnel, growling under his breath like a boar grizzly, mostly at himself for having left the log barricade open and his spear standing up against the cave wall. Anything could have wandered in, a bear or a badger or a skunk or even a cougar, looking for his cache of meat.

But it was no animal. The banshee, raging down the cañon, looking for him, had discovered his open tunnel. She roared in, tossing ash and sticks of firewood into the air, probing into his tunnels looking for him, clawing the dirt floor into whirlwinds until all was dark. The man barely had time to turn around before her long dry fingers discovered the coyote tunnel. She hissed and came for him, swelling up her cheeks and blowing loose dirt past him as he crawled and choked his way up toward the den and the opening and air. Hurrying to get ahead of him, she bashed him against the wall. It seemed for a moment he would suffocate right there, but he managed to get fingerholds on the floor and pull himself forward, and then he was in the den. But the banshee was there, too, making dry grass whirl and fly, pummeling him with small sticks and hunks of hard meat from the cache.

With one arm protecting his face, he groped with the other hand for the tunnel leading to the rock outcrop. When his hand suddenly plunged into emptiness, he followed it and found the upsloping way to the surface, to the air. There was the stone over the opening, but he pushed upward with all his strength and burst out to gasp a lungful of air. Before he took a second breath, he pulled himself free of the rocks and ran down the short slope to the open sage.

The banshee pursued, not with snow this time but with horrid shrieking howls, the screech of an eagle deprived of its prey. She soared over him, her face again growing out of the fast-flying cloud. She sped far ahead of him and bent her head downward like a monstrous wave curling over to scream into his face. But he would not turn from it. He stumbled on, falling to his knees and rising again, shielding his head with an arm, running straight into a sage bush and flying face first into the swirling sand. Again he rose and ran before her. She tore at his rags and twisted him around, but he recovered and struggled ahead. The farther he got from the cañon, the more the wind seemed to settle into a steady thrust behind him, still tripping him up and ripping at his rags, but pushing him forward. Exhausted, he managed to keep going, gasping for air. He came to the stage road, scarcely visible in the storm of flying sand, and there he tripped against something hard and went sprawling head-long into the earth. He wanted to give up, wanted only to lie there and rest, even if death was on his heels.

Then he looked and saw what had tripped him.

It was made of iron, sticking out of the blown sand in the middle of the stage tracks. A coupling link, lost from a passing freight wagon. A single, solitary iron link the length of a man's forearm. It was the same as the one the black-smith had handed him. It was a cold, hard, tangible reminder of his past, and it seemed to clear his mind.

Hard, cold, heavy, and real, it set thoughts into motion that had not been there for two years. The shrieking wind hammered at him, and he huddled there, losing consciousness. But before the darkness took him, he had a realization.

He knew the answer to the blacksmith's riddle.

When he woke, he wondered if he were dead. He lay on the cold earth among the sage, looking up into a fathomless black sky. A heavy full moon made the sage flats glow with eerie light. The banshee was no longer howling; in her place, a warmer wind flowed down from the mountains and off across the plain. It was a Chinook, softly warm and so gentle it hardly stirred the silvery branches of the moonstruck rabbitbrush. He sat up and saw the iron link next to him. For a long time he contemplated it. He looked up toward the distant mountains and out toward the eastern horizon, and he looked back toward the cañon. Finally he reached down and took up the iron link and began to walk north.

The link was heavy. He shifted it from hand to hand as he walked along in the wind-warmed moonlit night. Sometimes he tried carrying it on one shoulder, then the other. As the hours went by, the bright full moon paled and slid down behind the mountains while the eastern sky became lighter and lighter. On the eastern horizon a blood-red bulge began, as if molten lava were bursting from the prairie, and the bulge resolved itself into a glowing red disk floating free of the earth. The spreading sunlight warmed him. He walked on.

Shortly after sunrise he came across an abandoned sod hut, collapsed and overgrown, and, among the ruins of a pole shed, he found a forgotten rope, still coiled and hanging on a peg. It was old and dry and stiff, but he took it. He carefully tied one end to the iron link and wrapped the other end around his shoulders so he could drag the link behind him. And he went on that way, a hunched figure in rags and animal skins dragging an iron link behind him like a penitent on his way to be shriven.

He walked on. Sometimes he came to old snowfields not yet eaten up by the Chinook and gathered handfuls of snow to chew on as he walked. Sometimes he came to small arroyos with water running in them. On through the moonlight he explored the folds and pockets of his rags, and found scraps of jerked meat that he sucked on. Sometimes he would carry the link in two hands and study it thoughtfully, then lay it on the ground and drag it behind him. And so he went on, slowly using up his strength, gradually putting more distance between himself and the banshee cañon. With his feet wrapped up until they looked like big bundles of hide, and, with the link leaving a furrow in the dust, his meandering track resembled that of some huge lizard dragging its tail.

He grew weaker and weaker. In the end, he rested more than he walked, lying for hours in the dirt and finally rousing himself to go on. Inevitably there was no strength left in him. He was laboring up a small slope when he collapsed and could not rise again.

There he lay, an unconscious bundle of stinking hides and rags tethered by a rotten rope to an incongruous iron link. Just as he passed out, he imagined he could smell the smoke of a coal fire, the sulphur smell of a hot forge, and he wondered if the banshee had pursued him to the mouth of hell itself.

It was the boy who found him and brought the blacksmith, Evan Thompson, who stood towering over the bundle of smells and filth. He picked up the coupling link and untied it from its rope and tossed the heavy thing toward his forge as if it were no more than a pony shoe.

"He has solved the riddle," the blacksmith said to the boy. "Go and put the large boiler on the fire and fill it with water. I will bring him."

He hoisted Kyle to his shoulder and strode toward the camp where his wife stood waiting by a wagon. The forge smoldered near another wagon. They spread a wagon sheet, and Thompson kneeled on it to hold Kyle's head in his lap while the woman stripped him to the flesh and washed him with soap and warm water. She tenderly applied hot cloths to his face while the smith stropped his razor and whetted his shears. Then the smith held his head in his lap again and shaved him and cut his hair. Afterward they put fresh clothing on him, plain trousers and homespun shirt, a thick coat, a knitted cap. Then it was the woman's turn to cradle him while the smith spooned broth into his mouth, and in this way they restored him. Thompson placed him in the extra wagon and wrapped quilts around him, where he slept for two days with the boy keeping careful watch in case he woke.

On the third day he sat up and saw the boy. He lifted the edge of the wagon cover to look outside. The woman was there, kneading dough on the tailboard of the other wagon, and she smiled at him.

"Feeling strong enough to come to breakfast?" she said. "Or should I bring it to you?"

He could smell coffee.

"Think I can make it," he croaked. He felt his face with his hand. It was not only clean, but someone had shaved him. Someone had also cut his hair. His clothes were loose and clean and comfortable. He got out of the wagon and adjusted the knit cap and came to the fire with his hands in the pockets of the big coat.

" 'Morning." He mumbled like a man who'd just had a couple of teeth pulled. Or like someone with cotton wool packed into the back of his throat. It had been a long time. But although it took a while to get his mouth working, he soon spoke as though he had seen people every morning for the past two years. His mind felt strangely light and empty, free of dark thoughts and eager to receive news of the world of men.

"Good morning!" the blacksmith boomed. "Sit! Here's coffee."

The coffee scalded his parched lips and got into the open sores in his gums, but felt wonderful sliding down his throat. He couldn't get over how it felt to have something soft and sweet in his mouth, like flapjacks and honey, and he saw the boy smiling at him as he chewed and chewed each bite. Between bites he ran his hand over his bare chin or felt the back of his neck, amazed at how smooth it felt. Even his hands felt smooth and clean, and sometimes he looked down at them as if they belonged to someone else.

They ate in a curious kind of mutual understanding that there would be no questions, nothing said about what had transpired since the time they had met in town and now. Instead, he and Thompson spoke of the usual things that pass between men of the Western breed. Kyle mumbled compliments on the condition of the horses, and Thompson remarked that they were getting pretty old. He told the woman her biscuits and gravy were the best he had ever tasted, and she replied that it was only antelope venison gravy and she could do better with real beef. The boy finished eating and asked if he might go hunting, and Kyle admired his single-shot rifle and asked if he was a good shot.

Kyle did not ask what a blacksmith was doing so far out in the sage flats with his forge going at full heat. The blacksmith did not ask what Kyle was doing lying on a hill in rags, tied to an iron link. Neither man asked, because both men knew.

Afterward, as the woman was washing the tin plates at her tub, Kyle and the blacksmith went to the forge to warm their hands and talk. A big tarp had been rigged up like a lean-to to keep the wind off the forge, and under the tarp lay Thompson's chain, the chain he seemed never to finish. Another link lay in the coals, apparently waiting to be added to the rest.

"I guess I'll need to beg your hospitality another day or two," Kyle said. "Don't quite feel up t' walking to the Keystone just yet."

The smith selected a flat bar of steel and thrust it into the coals, more out of habit than because he wanted to make anything of it.

"You will be with us a good deal longer," he said. "You need to be strengthened. Take hold of the bellows there."

Kyle grasped the long handle and bore down on it, but it barely moved. A very tiny puff of air stirred the coal fire.

"Too weak to go anywhere. So, you'll stay here and you'll eat. You'll pump the bellows. You need to get used to riding again, and you need a strong back and arms."

"Well," Kyle said, "that'll all come back once I get to the Keystone. Doesn't ever take me long to get into shape."

"You're not going back to the Keystone Ranch, not yet."

"I'm not?"

"No. You first have a job to do out there," the big blacksmith said, pointing northeast. "Some men have built a fort and a settlement. They are keeping a woman there, and you are to go and get her. You must take her to the Keystone."

"By myself? I haven't even held a gun in I don't know how long."

"It can only be done by one man. You will have a gun, but you won't use it."

Into the silence between them, there rose the sound of geese calling to one another as they flew northward in ragged formations, returning with the spring as it moved north ahead of them in the timeless ritual of freeze and thaw, of dormancy and awakening.

Kyle stayed with the blacksmith. His strength grew. He pumped the bellows, hammered iron, cut firewood with the smith's massive axe. Sometimes he took the shotgun and went with the boy to hunt sage hens and deer. The blacksmith moved camp from time to time, and, while Kyle could never discern why they had moved, he did see that the direction was always northeast.

When they camped near a creek, he carried buckets of water to fill the barrels. The blacksmith went with him to the creek and filled each bucket half full and ordered Kyle to lift them above his head, over and over. A week of this, and more water was put into the buckets, and more, until they were full and he could swing both of them straight up and hold them aloft. Every day the blacksmith would point to something else and challenge Kyle to try lifting it. Kyle's chest swelled proudly when he first lifted a sack of coal overhead, then two sacks at the same time. After a week of coal sacks, he could hoist a keg of iron nails, first to his knees, then to his waist, and then one day all the way over his head. It was that evening when Kyle told the smith how he had dug the burrow in the cañon. He told him about the banshee and the sounds in the earth, and Thompson listened with interest.

One day the smith put his back to the wagon. He gripped the step and lifted the hind wheels off the ground.

He laughed and dared Kyle to do it, but Kyle could not. But each evening after supper, Kyle went to the wagon and heaved against the weight, certain that the day would come when he could.

The horseback practice came easily to him once the good food had restored his energy, and, although the smith's horses were large and heavy and there was no saddle except for the boy's small saddle that he used on his light pony, Kyle could soon ride as well as ever. He would swing up on one of the big horses, the boy would mount his pony, and the two of them would race. His legs became hard and strong from gripping the horse's flanks, and supple enough that he could spring up onto its back with ease.

One day when he and the boy came racing back toward the wagons after a long ride, he saw the smith standing there with a sack of coal cradled in one huge arm.

The smith beckoned Kyle toward him.

Kyle smiled and kicked the horse into a fast run, laying himself low over the neck like a race jockey, charging the big man. As he came almost abreast, the smith suddenly threw the bag of coal at Kyle's chest. He caught it, and it sent him toppling over the horse's haunches into a yucca plant.

"Once more," the smith said, retrieving the sack of coal but doing nothing to help Kyle up out of the bayonet plant. Kyle limped after the horse, mounted, and came charging back, this time more cautiously.

"Faster!" the smith roared, making the horse startle.

Again he threw the coal sack, and again and again and all through the following days, until Kyle could come at full speed and catch the heavy, lumpy sack and ride off with it draped across the horse in front of him. Occasionally he would even throw it back to the smith. If the smith held the sack, rather than tossing it, Kyle could come by and snatch it from his grip, wheel, toss it back again.

All summer he grew in strength and agility. Always the woman was there, the blacksmith's wife, glad to wash the coal dust and dirt from his shirt, smiling to feed him second helpings of her venison stew or the sage hen she baked beneath the fire coals. She always had some stew or beans simmering in a Dutch oven down in the bean hole pit next to the fire. One night she studied his face intently, and the next evening she presented him with a new eye patch, shaped and sewn from kid leather to fit snugly over his bad eye. The cord was woven in a fine round braid, slender and strong.

All I need now, he thought, *is a good horse, a Stetson, and a Colt, and I'll be back to where I was.*

Dark nights still brought the dreams that made him sweat and twist, and chills shivered up his spine when storm clouds drifted overhead. Evan Thompson moved camp to a gorge where he could hack coal from an exposed seam, and, although the coal tunnel was shallow, Kyle could not force himself to enter it. He waited outside, filling gunny sacks with the chunks of coal tossed out by the smith.

"No taste for mining?" Thompson said.

"Let's say I spent enough time in a hole," Kyle replied.

"That's a shame," Thompson said, "because you have another dark hole ahead of you."

Kyle looked into the low, rectangular hole Thompson had chipped into the coal seam over the years.

"The grave, you mean?"

Thompson, taken by surprise, chuckled. "That, too," he said. "But later on."

So Kyle Owen, traveling on the seat of Thompson's wagon, had fears for the future to add to the nightmares from the past. Had the blacksmith saved his life and given him back his strength just so he could spend another two years in some dark hole in the ground?

Thompson moved camp twice more, and it was late summer, but not yet autumn, when Kyle's horse, Stetson, and Colt appeared. They came in the keeping of a man who wore a black coat and came riding into camp at midday in the manner of a range rider looking for supper. But this stranger was not hungry, nor was he courteous. In addition to a holstered Colt, he carried a shotgun across the pommel of his saddle and a sneer across his face.

"Blacksmith," he said, "I'm sent to tell you to come no closer. All this range is staked and claimed by the brothers. We don't like trespassers."

"I know."

"Brother Arbeit doesn't want you camping on the brothers' land. The council sent me to tell you."

The smith turned to Kyle as if the dark rider didn't exist. "They call him Brother Arbeit," Thompson explained, "but in fact he is more like General Arbeit or King Arbeit. A fat and tiresome religious tyrant.

"Tell me," Thompson said to the rider, "has Arbeit returned from Salt Lake yet? Or did *Brother* Young's Avenging Angels hang him?"

The rider's face reddened with rage. "You shut your mouth, smith!" he said.

The smith went on talking to Kyle.

"These are the Brothers of the Received Light," he explained, "led by this Arbeit. He considers himself to be the only true prophet of what they call Latter-Day Saints. He and some other self-deluded misfits . . . like this one . . . went into schism with the church, started their own colony. They began by seizing the Great North project from two women. They diverted the water into their own ditch system up in the hills. Apparently God said the water was theirs. Arbeit talks to God, you know. Unless Young's avengers strung him up to a cottonwood limb."

"You're diggin' your grave with your mouth," the rider growled. "You don't wanna mess with the council. An' they told me t' tell you t' git off this range!"

With that, he wheeled his horse and trotted back the way he had come, stiffly proud. Or scared. Thompson looked after him.

"You were saying something about a gun?" Thompson said to Kyle, nodding toward the departing rider.

"Maybe I found one," Kyle said.

The brother heard the heavy clopping of the wagon horse coming behind him, but did not move the shotgun from its position across his saddle. He only turned his head indifferently to sneer at the clean-shaven Kyle. An unarmed man coming up beside him, wearing a farmer's coat and stocking hat, riding bareback on a draft horse.

The brother began to say—"And what do *you* want?"—when he felt himself seized by the collar and belt, lifted from the saddle, and flopped across the other horse. Kyle relieved him of the revolver and shotgun in one smooth movement. Carrying the unfortunate enforcer across the draft horse like a sack of potatoes, Kyle took him back to the wagons and dumped him on the ground. Kyle dismounted and stood over him with the shotgun aimed at his belt buckle.

"Now," Kyle said, "let's see how quick you can strip."

The dark Stetson fit him well, but the boots were a little loose, and the like-new California pants were a trifle short. The shotgun had seen use, but the Colt .45 didn't even show holster wear on the bluing. The saddle was good, and underneath the assorted plunder in the saddlebags there were two full boxes of shells.

As for the brother, he went limping across the sage, hurrying as much as a barefoot man can hurry through cactus country.

The woman and boy began rolling up blankets and tarps and stowing cooking gear in boxes. Thompson dug a hole and buried the hot coals of his forge, then rummaged around in one of the boxes and came up with a pair of moccasins, good ones with hard buffalo skin soles. He beckoned to the boy.

"Our visitor has gotten the point by now," he told him. "Get your pony and take these to him. No use torturing a man just for delivering messages. They're going to be hard enough on him when he gets home."

The boy was back in just over an hour. He still had the moccasins, tied by their strings and looped over his saddle horn.

"Gone," he said. "I followed his tracks, and all of a sudden they turned kinda south and stopped next to a wagon track. Looks like he got a ride."

"Probably knew where the road was," Kyle said. "I'd do the same. Could you tell which way the wagon was headed?"

The boy beamed proudly. "I got down and studied on that," he said. "From the horse tracks, I figure it had two teams, at least, and was headed pretty much south."

"He's running away," Thompson observed. "I wondered if maybe he'd do that."

"These Brothers of the Whatever," Kyle said, "not too loyal to the cause?"

"Depends," Thompson said. "Some probably came

along from Salt Lake, hoping to get themselves better land, a new start, or get away from some situation. Not for the religion of it. Some might have come because some wife or relative wanted them to. That book you found in the saddlebag, now, some of them get to reading it and decide they can't stake their immortal soul on what it says."

The book was small and cheaply bound, and the pages were gray paper with blurry type. The inside page said it was THE SACRED WORD OF RECEIVED ENLIGHTENMENT. The next page said it was the "True Testament of a Revelation Handed Down to The Latter-Day Saints By Means of Enlightenment Through Two Holy Vessels and Witnesses." The Holy Vessels turned out to be Brother Bishop Arbeit and another bishop, Brother Herzchen. Kyle kept it in the saddlebag, thinking it might be something to pass the time with.

The sun was high as they made their start. Kyle rode apart, ranging in the sage for a shot at a prairie chicken or rabbit for the pot. The sun beat warmly on him, and the fresh light seemed to purify the light green of the sage and the darker green of the scrub juniper. The sandy soil itself seemed golden and untouched in the sunlight. Whatever this dark hole was that Thompson said was waiting for him, it didn't seem to be anywhere around here.

He rode a trio of fat prairie hens up out of a draw and brought two of them down with the shotgun. It was enough. Kyle rode back toward the wagons, only to find that Thompson had shifted course and was now moving in a more westward direction. Kyle caught up and pointed in the direction from which the brother had come.

"Thought we were goin' that way," he said.

"To their compound?" the smith said. "Far too many of them. We need a diversion to get them out of there. And

I've got an idea for that. We'll go this way."

Kyle sometimes rode ahead, sometimes rode a wide circle around the two wagons partly to be sure they had not been followed, partly to exercise the horse, and mostly out of a newly remembered joy in the feeling of a good horse and saddle under him once more. Sometimes he rode beside the second wagon and talked with the boy who was driving, but the boy was not much of a conversationalist.

They made cold camp that night and went on the next day. Kyle read THE RECEIVED WORD, or whatever it was.

They followed the foothills and camped again. Kyle went on reading.

"Interesting?" Thompson asked.

"More like strange. A lot of it don't make sense. It sounds like somebody tryin' to write a Bible for himself. But you know, it feels good t' be reading words again. Been a long time since I saw a book."

"You keep on. That book could be more use to you than the shotgun when you get to their settlement."

"Hah?"

"Hasn't dawned on you yet, I see. That man who came to warn us, he didn't go back to them. You'll arrive wearing their kind of clothes. They'll take you for a messenger from Salt Lake, I'm thinking."

"You're forgettin' the horse," Kyle said.

"Pretty ordinary animal," Thompson said. "But I've got some leather dye we could put on that white blaze."

"So they just open the gates and let me in?"

"It'll help if you recite a few lines from that book. Something like . . . 'Lo, I am among thee with manna and myrrh.' I doubt if it has to make sense."

Kyle grinned. "Kind of like the book is mightier than the Colt, is that it?"

Evan Thompson shook his head. "Keep reading," he said.

Some part of Kyle's mind was totally at ease with this life of slow moving days and calm evenings, while another part of him itched to be doing something. He hunted, which at least took him away from the wagons for a while, but it was not enough.

At last the small caravan came in sight of a deep gorge leading into the mountains. A faint wagon track labored up the slope beside it. It doubled back on itself three times and crossed a sloping meadow and finally brought them out on the rim of the cañon. Kyle dismounted and stood at the edge looking down on the brothers' handiwork, a sturdy irrigation flume made out of milled lumber. It was part of a ditch system that ran up the gorge as far as he could see, and downward toward the plains.

Incredibly they had diverted the Great North project. With the energy and determination religious fervor can often inspire, they had drilled into the granite and moved tons of rock to take the water to the dry sage flats. Like the ditch, the flume was as wide as a wagon bed.

The blacksmith set up camp, and after supper he and Kyle walked the edge of the cañon to study the brothers' irrigation project. A gentle wind stirred the pines, and the small birds of late afternoon chirruped to one another in the branches. The scent of pine filled the air, and the mountain shadows lay deep in the cañon.

Kyle looked down, and Thompson saw him shiver involuntarily.

"Does this bother you? The height?"

"No," Kyle replied.

"Maybe you were thinking of the cañon where you spent the winter. You and your ghosts."

"These are different ghosts," Kyle said.

"Oh," Thompson said. "The ditch. I understand."

"I killed men because of that water. Seems like I forgot who I was and where I'd come from, up there at Crannog. There was that foreman I had t' kill . . . a guardian she called him . . . and she made me take his place. All because of that water."

Shadows and phantoms clouded his thoughts, ghostly images of long days spent riding the ditch. Hot summer days and freezing nights, endless hours of boredom, and sudden times of deadly violence.

"Men have killed each other for water from the beginning of time," Thompson said. "Up at Crannog you were protecting the very source of the water itself. It's a small wonder that you were taken over by it."

"That's it," Kyle said. "Taken over. I never want to be that way again."

"That's in the future," Thompson said. "Right now we need to break some holes in the ditch down there. I think we can do it so that it will look like natural causes. Landslides. Most of the brothers will come up here to repair it, and you will be able to enter their compound."

"So," Kyle said, still gazing into the evening shadows cloaking the cañon with darkness. "What's your plan?"

Chapter Ten

THE POWER OF THE WORD

"This is a good time for it," the big blacksmith said.

They were riding the ridge above the flume, following it upstream to the irrigation ditch that cut through the mountains.

"Their crops are up but are not ready for harvest. Seeing their ditches go dry will bring them hurrying up here to the cañon like swarming ants."

"So where are we goin' to be when they come?" Kyle asked.

"Far from here! My travels lead to the Pecos River, south of here, through the mountains. You should cross over the river after we have done our mischief, so you can approach the compound from the north."

Kyle took off the dark Stetson and wiped the sweatband.

"The *hombre* who owned this hat," he said. "Y' suppose he went back to his friends and has 'em up in arms and ready for me?"

"I doubt it!" Thompson laughed. "If he had, they would have found us by now. They no doubt went looking for him when he did not return, but by then he was far away and we were long gone."

"What if they found our tracks? Your wagons leave 'em pretty plain."

"Would they follow them into the mountains more than a day's ride from their compound? I think they would be glad to see we were heading away from their settlement."

Kyle left Thompson with the horses and descended the nearly perpendicular slope by hanging to branches and bushes. He crossed the ditch on a foot-log and walked the embankment, looking for just the right place to do the mischief. The way it reminded him of patrolling the Great North ditch gave him an eerie feeling, a tingle crawling up his backbone. He watched the woods, half expecting to see Luned's ghostly white form vanishing among the trees, or that misshapen dark creature that protected the gates.

Most of this ditch traversed steep slopes, winding in and out with the terrain. Within a mile, Kyle found the sort of place he was looking for. They had logged the trees here, probably for flume timbers, and the ground showed where they had dragged them downhill. Rain had made gullies out of the furrows, and animals had grazed the grass down to the roots. Above this steep acre of ruin, several large boulders clung precariously to the slope, just waiting for a heavy rainstorm to send them sliding.

From his seasons as the Great North ditch guardian, Kyle knew this situation all too well: inevitably the rain and snow and freezing would dislodge a boulder, which would start a small landslide, which would fill the ditch with a ton of dirt and rock. If no one discovered it in time, the water would back up, wash out a hole in the embankment, and go pouring down into the cañon, taking out hundreds of feet of ditch.

Kyle hiked back down the ditch to find Thompson studying another weak spot in the water project. It was a narrow side cañon coming down into the valley, and, while it was narrow, it was both deep and steep. To span it the builders had built a wooden flume on log trestles. They had taken the nearest trees to use for supports; the stumps were still visible in the now nude side cañon. All that remained in the steep gorge were scrawny chokecherry and manzanita bushes.

Climbing up into the narrow cleft, Kyle and Thompson found a thick section of log, thicker than those in the trestle. It was limbed and ready to go, but the brothers had left it behind.

"Probably didn't need it," Kyle said.

"Might have been too big for their purposes," Thompson said. "But it suits ours. We'll use those thick branches for levers."

The two men muscled the heavy length of tree trunk down the gorge until they could swivel it and anchor it behind stumps on either side. Stripped to the waist, they wrestled boulders and small stones down against the log until they had several tons of granite ready to go tumbling into the narrow draw and smash the flume trestle.

With food and drink, the boy came to find them. After eating, they rested themselves and put the boy to gathering dry brush and pitch-pine knots. Thompson showed the boy how to stack the tinder under the center of the log. With the updraft in the gorge, it would make a hot fire and would quickly burn through the log.

Farther up the ditch they built another rockslide, piling boulders against a log right alongside the ditch.

"When this one goes," Kyle said, stacking twigs and brush under the supporting log, "all this rock'll just plop into th' water. Won't break the ditch open, but it'll sure back it up. Somewhere up above, she'll eventually give way."

When they had finished, they washed in the freezing water. Kyle saw the sunlight dancing on the ripples of the flowing stream like scattered diamonds. Thompson looked at the stack of rock behind the log and the kindling stuffed underneath it and laughed his booming laugh.

"Do you see it?" he asked.

"See what?"

"How it all depends on all the parts. One little Lucifer match lights a twig. A small burning stick sets fire to a larger one and another, and the log burns through. One rock starts rolling. Just one rock is not enough, but it can jar another. Two of them moving together can unseat a third, and so on and so on. It is like the chain. One link alone has no purpose, no matter how well made. Each depends on the other."

Kyle grinned and wiped his face with his shirt, then put it on. The sun warmed his back. It was time to go back to camp and eat and rest.

The sun was flooding the upper sky with light but had not yet risen high enough to pour through the forest and dissipate the light fog when they broke camp and packed up the gear. Thompson sent the boy and woman on ahead with the heavier wagon. He and Kyle watched them vanish along the dim trail into the morning mountain mist. Thompson would light the bonfire under the log, and then follow them in the light wagon.

Kyle sat in the saddle, ready to ride up and set the other fire and cross over the cañon to start down toward the compound. The blacksmith offered his hand.

"See y' again, sometime," Kyle said.

"Yes," the smith said, "we'll fire up a forge together."

"That link . . . ," Kyle began.

"Yes?"

"I got it right, didn't I? The riddle?"

"You did, rider," the big blacksmith replied. "You did. I told you so, down there on the ditch."

With a wave of his hand, Evan Thompson was gone into the misty trees, heading toward the little side cañon. Kyle turned his horse and rode the other direction. Whatever he was supposed to do from now on, whatever lay in front of him, it began now. He felt it in his soul and through every muscle of his body, and it was a feeling more welcome than any he could remember. Sunlight found an opening in the morning mist and came flooding through, battering the forest and mountain with life.

Only the two of them, looking back, knew what the thin threads of smoke rising in the mountains meant. Only two men heard the faraway cañon echoes of landslides. One was on a wagon driving southward, following a long-deserted track; the other was north of the cañon on a ridge, sitting tall and dark in the saddle.

The crash and rumble startled the cañon deer that went springing over fallen logs and bouncing up the slope. Small birds stopped chittering over their seeds and flew into higher trees. Hawks and an eagle rose suddenly on the morning air. They had all heard it. First there was the cracking noise of a log breaking, then the rolling thunder of granite rocks booming down a narrow gorge, slowly at first and then speeding up in clouds of dust and duff, undercutting other rocks, bringing them along, the mass now bouncing and flowing at the same time, treetops shaking so that needles and cones came loose to join the obdurate, resistless downward chaos of rock. The very first boulders, the heavy leaders, hardly slowed down as they broke the flume supports at ground level. The timbers flew up, toppled back, twisted and cracked where they connected to the planks and crosspieces. Planks, supports, braces, and beams—in an instant all became a pile of splintered lumber pulverized by the rolling landslide.

The water came pouring off the ruined flume in a long waterfall, carrying rock and timbers and all into the bottom of the cañon. There the big rocks remained, rolling over and over but, piece by piece, coming to rest under the torrent while the lighter dirt and sand and twigs and planks and logs joined water in a thick muddy tongue thrusting from the mouth of the cañon, headed toward the settlement on the sage plain.

After two hours, the second log finally burned through. As Kyle had said, the rocks sloughed down into the ditch and blocked it completely. But the water kept coming. It rose behind the boulders and dirt, rose to the top of the embankment, spread back upditch, and increased to enormous weight as it rose, putting irresistible pressure against the restraining dikes.

It finally broke through far upstream of the blockage, and the drainage of countless slopes and valleys ran down the cañon in one overpowering body of water.

Kyle took care to circle widely around the settlement, concealing himself in an arroyo. He wanted to ride closer and see the damage they had done, but he knew he must be patient. It took time to send men to find out what had happened, and even more time to organize work parties to fix it.

For two nights he slept warmly wrapped in the slicker and blanket the brother had thoughtfully left strapped to the saddle. The third day he crawled close enough to be able to see figures moving around at the settlement. He acted with the same stealth he had used when he trailed the coyotes and wolves to steal their kills. He could sit against a scrub cedar for hours until he seemed to be part of it.

He crept from concealment to concealment with the patience of a wolf stalking a prairie hen, learning every feature of the landscape, studying the settlement from nearly every angle. The river was on the far side, and a few rough cabins stood near the bank. There was a crossing there, but the flood had ruined it. A crude road led from the crossing, between the cabins, past a pair of larger houses, and into the compound. This was the adobe fortress he had heard about—in actuality, just a plain adobe wall surrounding squat adobe buildings. The road went in through a wide gateway; on the far side was another wide gateway leading into a corral that contained a small herd of horses and a couple of milk cows.

The community had planted most of their crops across the river and irrigated them from a small reservoir fed by the ditch. Now the reservoir was brown mud, and a few women were wading in the flooded furrows, trying to salvage something. A man on a plow horse went riding up toward the cañon. The river crossing between settlement and fields was gouged out completely, but a rope had been rigged as a hand line so people could wade across in the mud.

There were only a few horses left in the corrals, and he spotted only a few men walking around. The blacksmith had figured it right; they had all hurried up the cañon like ants to repair the damage as quickly as possible. To them, that was the most important thing. To Kyle the important thing was that damned few of them had bothered to stay at home.

The next morning, he rode in.

A boy not yet in his teens was on duty at the corral, standing watch. What he saw coming was a man riding a good horse, wearing a black coat and dark wide-brimmed hat under which he wore a gun belt. The rider's pants were dark as well. A double-barreled shotgun stuck out of a scabbard behind the saddle. As he came closer, the rider took out a small black book, and the boy recognized it.

Kyle rode straight up to the corral so deliberately that the boy hurried to open the gate for him. He rode among the livestock, looking at the horses. He rode over and examined a heavy buckboard standing under a lean-to roof. Satisfied, he turned to the boy and spoke.

"Pick out your best team and hitch 'em up to that rig," he said.

The boy touched the brim of his floppy hat and went to do as he was told.

Kyle rode to the opposite gate, leaned over to flip open the loop, and rode on into the compound. Small children stopped playing to stare at him. Two old men came out of a low adobe building and stood looking. A half dozen women, wearing black dresses and bonnets, came out and stood huddled together, waiting for him to speak. He held the black book out toward them.

" 'And the angel saith unto them, verily amongst thee is one who is not of thee but with thee. Bring her before me!' "

The old men joined the women, and they all continued to stare mutely at the dark figure on horseback. The children drew back into the shadow of a low porch.

Kyle simply sat there. He had learned this from watching the wolves—if a wolf happened to come upon a deer that was lying down and resting, instead of lunging forward, the wolf would merely sit back on its haunches and stare and stare until the deer seemed to go into some kind of trance. And then the wolf had him.

After a minute or two of mute suspicion and resistance,

the tallest woman went up to the building and drew back
the bar bolting the door. She opened the door and beckoned, and a slender woman in pale yellow stepped,
blinking, into the sunshine.

It was Luned.

Luned. She raised her eyes and saw him. And knew him.
He looked into her face without emotion, although his mind
again heard her accusations and felt the slash of the quirt
across his cheek. That moment stood between them now,
and the moment tried to infuriate her into fleeing back into
the dark building, preferring captivity to rescue by this man.
The moment probed Kyle's anger, trying to break the hard-
jawed calm that was his only armor against the massed
brothers.

She stood, calmly regarding him as if his coming was no
surprise to her.

The tension weakened. It rose from his shoulders and
drifted off in the sun, and she saw him in his full courage.
And he saw her as she truly was, unarmed and small. Her
eyes and the set of her chin showed bravery and stubborn
determination, but he was in charge of the situation. He
had to be, for it to work.

Kyle pointed the black book at her.

" 'And it is written let not the daughters of Pisgah lie
down with the saints of the redeemed!' " he thundered.
" 'Yea, I am sent to thee for accounting'!"

He had read that in the book. He held the book like a
pistol and pointed it first at one person and then another,
and he took secret glee in the way it made them shrink and
step back.

Two men in black shirts and trousers walked in through
the gate of the compound and stood in front of Kyle's
horse. He figured they had been waiting outside the wall

and had heard everything. He turned his steady gaze on them.

One of them began speaking. "She," he said, pointing at Luned, "she killed two of the brothers."

"When? Why?" Kyle boomed.

"It was . . . we were told to go to that irrigation project. Two, three summers back. I don't know. Told t' bust the ditch and get water for the settlement. This'n killed two of our men."

"You brought her here?"

"No! Not us! The bishop, he sent men after her. Found 'er last winter, hidin' at the railroad town."

"Arbeit." Kyle scowled and drew the shotgun from the scabbard and laid it across his knees.

"Yeah."

"Where is he, the bishop?"

"Just got back from Salt Lake, two days ago. He's up to the cañon with th' other men t' fix the break in the ditch."

"Why is the woman still alive?" Kyle asked. "Surely the vengeance of the Lord should have been visited upon her." He was enjoying his play-acting.

"She's being converted. God's truth . . . one of the women reads the gospel to her every single day. Brother Arbeit says he'll take her to wife, once she sees the light."

Kyle opened the book and made a show of looking for a particular passage in order to keep secret the rueful smile that threatened to destroy his mask.

" 'Whosoever shall do murder among thee, so shalt he be judged by the highest of the prophets, who are of the power given unto them by God'." It didn't make much sense, but sounded Biblical as all hell.

A horseman appeared at the gateway, and, some distance behind him, Kyle saw a troop of maybe twenty men on horseback coming toward the compound. They reined up outside the gateway with faces showing confusion and consternation. They seemed to be waiting for something. Or someone.

Kyle wasn't going to sit there while they waited, however. He turned his horse toward the two old men.

"You two," he said. "Help the boy hitch a team to that buckboard. Then back it in here. You," he said, pointing the book at Luned, "you get your things together, if you got any, and put them in the wagon."

He waved the book again for dramatic effect so the riders outside the gate could see.

" 'For great and ancient mysteries are given unto the prophets and I am sent for the Strange One even to deliver her before the altar of Revelation'!" All those days listening to Evan Thompson's booming bombast were now paying off.

Luned looked into his face, and he knew the past was over. Whatever had happened to him during his two winters alone, something had also happened to her, and they were as two ancient acquaintances thrust into a new beginning. Without a word she quickly disappeared into the building.

Kyle turned and studied the young man who had not spoken. The other one, the one who was so anxious to volunteer information, was the weak member of a coyote pack, the one who hangs back in a fight, ready to jump to the side of whichever bunch of animals looks like it's winning. The silent man interested Kyle more. He was Kyle's own size, but even more muscular through the shoulders. He stood tall and straight and watchful. When this man looked at his uncertain brothers clustered together outside the gate, Kyle saw independence in his face, a sense of pride and cold superiority. He was not intimidated, either by Kyle or by the mounted men at the gate.

Kyle felt an instant kinship with him.

"You," Kyle said. "Stand over here. What's your name?"

"It's Emil."

"Help the woman with her things, when they get the buckboard here."

Emil looked at the one-eyed rider with detached interest, looked at his fellows bunched up outside the gate, and went inside the building to find Luned.

Kyle rode to the gateway and silently confronted the group. A lone rider was coming, and, from the way the others turned to look in that direction, he figured it was the bishop himself. So he would wait. He slid the shotgun back into the scabbard, out of the way, and opened his book to a turned-down page.

It didn't take much looking to see that Brother Arbeit was one of those puffed-up, little tyrants whose clothes seem like they ought to belong to a bigger man. Red-faced and still shaking from his bouncing ride down the hill, he bustled to the front of the pack, overflowing with self-importance. Kyle had only to glance over the top of the book to size him up. Fat face covered with a black beard, a huge hat, oversize black coat, a gun belt cinched around his fat stomach, high boots with his pants tucked in. *A real leader of men,* Kyle sneered to himself.

Kyle spoke first. "I have come for her," he said.

Like the rest of the flock, Brother Arbeit assumed that Kyle was one of Salt Lake's notorious Avenging Angels sent to police the outlying settlements. Such men were said to ride in groups of six, and it was rumored that six of them could withstand an armed force five times their size. To make matters worse, Brother Arbeit realized, only a few of his followers were carrying guns. Most of their weapons were inside the thick-walled building. They had gone into the cañon to repair the ditch, and a gun belt got in a man's way when he worked. Contrary to the rumors, they were farmers with families, not fighting men. They had no time to practice shooting. Hardly any of them could afford ammunition, even if they had a place to buy it. He did have two armed wardens, but one had vanished and the other was still up in the cañon.

Brother Arbeit knew how weak his position was. The strange woman shouldn't be in his compound. She was only there because she had bewitched him somehow. She scorned him at every turn, yet, in her body, he sensed a kind of carnal promise. Even the way she walked made him want to wive her. In Salt Lake, he had not dared to mention her, lest the council see the lust in his eyes.

Arbeit wished he had a more imposing army to back him up, some fierce-looking black-coated men with rifles and shotguns to make this dark stranger think twice before doing anything. Instead, his army was a clot of farmers in shirtsleeves and coveralls sitting there like they were embarrassed.

Unsure of his supporters, Arbeit decided that his best hope lay in using his air of authority to bluff his way to the armory. It had intimidated others and might intimidate the man with the eye patch.

"Welcome, stranger," he said in his lowest voice, his artificial smile straining his face muscles. "Will you enter into our compound and break bread with us?" He tried to say it like a command.

Kyle raised his eye from his book and looked around as if he were reminding himself of where he was. Or as if trying to see where the sound was coming from.

"Seems like I'm the one who's in," Kyle said. "You are outside."

Two little beads of sweat ran down into Brother Arbeit's heavy beard. Still he went on talking. He tried to smile.

"As you are one of us, I am pleased to welcome you into our little community," he said.

Kyle looked him up and down as if the bishop had said the stupidest thing on earth. And then Kyle held up the book and spoke again.

" 'Behold an evil one did desire the throne of Nothol and did lead an uprising until the commandment of God was that he be struck down and all who did join with him'."

Kyle waited. His eye studied the group, one by one, taking all the time in the world. More than one of them looked down at the ground. His assessment of Emil had been right; the young man didn't belong with this bunch of sheep. Brother Arbeit's forehead and cheeks simmered red, soaking his beard with sweat.

"Are there others with you?" Arbeit asked.

Kyle smiled at him, much as a wolf seems to smile while tossing a crippled gopher into the air and catching it, toying with it before snapping its jaws shut on the neck. The long silence was broken by the shuffling of horse's hoofs and the sounds of the buckboard being backed into the compound behind him.

Bishop Arbeit finally mustered himself. He sat up as tall as he could and rode forward. His followers didn't move.

"I have business to attend to," he said brusquely. "You are welcome to eat with us, if you choose to stay. . . ." He stopped abruptly when he saw the loaded wagon and Luned standing beside it. She had helped herself to a considerable stock of supplies and bedding. The two folds of fat under his chin turned red with indignation.

"You, there!" Arbeit yelled. "What are you doing?!"

Kyle swung his horse to block Arbeit's, and they sat

glaring at each other, Arbeit casting anxious glances toward Luned and back again to Kyle. The bishop considered going for his gun, but, when he looked at the way Kyle's Colt hung strapped to his leg, he reconsidered. He thought of calling up some of his men to go with him into the compound, but he was not sure how they would react. He thought of riding a wide circle around this threatening figure, but to do so would look cowardly. Finally he spoke.

"That woman," he said, pointing, "is the enemy of our church. A murderess."

Kyle continued to look into the bishop's face. "What's she doing here?" he quietly asked. "You did not send her to Salt Lake for punishment? You made no mention of her in Salt Lake?"

It was a guess, a bluff, but seemed like a logical one. Kyle figured Arbeit had made his trip to Salt Lake so he could bluster and get recognition, and the last thing he'd do was tell them about a pretty young infidel, a female gentile hidden at his compound.

"How did you know that?" Arbeit sweated. "I only returned two days ago."

" 'The eyes of the prophets are everywhere'," Kyle said, " 'and the voice reacheth all ears, verily even the ears of the avenger'." He put the book into the pocket of his black coat with an air of finality.

The bishop didn't exactly recall those words from the BOOK OF THE RECEIVED LIGHT, but he wasn't about to argue about it. Kyle waited for his next move.

Seeing Luned climbing onto the seat of the buckboard, Arbeit kicked his horse forward and swept his coat open to show his gun in its shoulder holster. He would not lose her, even if it meant physically forcing the dark rider out of his way.

As he came stirrup to stirrup with the one-eyed man, thinking he would brush past, he felt himself lifted out of the saddle and slammed down again, so hard that it knocked the breath out of him.

Kyle had reached over, got himself a handful of black coat lapel, and jerked Bishop Arbeit clean out of the saddle. He dropped him facedown in front of him and held him there with one hand while he reached into the bishop's coat and took charge of the revolver. He calmly broke it open, checked the loads, snapped it shut, and put the muzzle to the back of the bishop's neck.

"Guns," he said to the few brothers who had weapons on them. "Unload 'em. Throw 'em over there."

Seeing their leader over this stranger's saddle, the bishop's own gun pointed at the base of his skull, the men complied. They dragged out their assortment of pistols and obligingly emptied the cartridges onto the ground before tossing the guns into a pile next to the adobe wall. Kyle called to the man named Emil and told him to collect the weapons.

"Toss 'em in the horse trough," he said, "and fetch some rope."

Deciding not to take the chance that some brother might be a hero, Kyle tucked the bishop's gun into his belt and took out his shotgun.

"Now," he said, "you boys just turn around backwards in the saddle. I want to see every one of you facin' your horse's rear-end. And don't touch ground doin' it."

It was comic, this picture of twenty men awkwardly trying to turn around in the saddle, but it was soon accomplished. In the process, some of the horses had danced around so that the riders were facing Kyle again, but sitting ass-backward. They could only watch while Kyle rode over

154

to the buckboard and plopped the bishop on the back of it so his legs dangled down. He beckoned to Emil.

"Tie his hands behind him," he said. "Then his feet. Then take the end of your rope down around the axle and tie it off."

The bishop was soon hog-tied like a pig ready for market, sitting on the tail of the buckboard, glaring and sweating. Emil added his own frightening touch, which was to loop the rope around Arbeit's neck before tying it to the axle. Arbeit had now become Luned's hostage; if she whipped up the horses suddenly, he would tumble off the wagon and be dragged by the neck, hands and feet tied. Kyle looked into Emil's face and made a slight nod in acknowledgement of mutual understanding. Emil would not remain here. His strength and independence marked him too deeply.

Kyle touched the brim of his hat to Emil and turned to Luned.

"Head out," he said.

Emil stood aside as Luned clucked to the team and drove the loaded buckboard through the corral and down the two-rut road, leading north, her well-trussed hostage swaying and scooting his butt around to stay on. Kyle went back to the group of backward-mounted men who were sitting, sullen and silent, like a bunch of schoolboys being punished. He pulled out his book.

" 'Now behold, this giveth my soul sorrow,' said Jacob. 'Those who doeth iniquity shall be led away. One wicked man can causeth great wickedness to take place among the children of man.' First you must repair thy ditches. Then, you must choose one among you to send to the council for their orders."

Kyle figured it would take them all winter to fix the

ditch. A month to choose a new leader. Even if they picked somebody and sent him tomorrow, by the time he got all the way to Salt Lake City and back, Kyle and Luned would be back at the Keystone.

Kyle deliberately spurred his horse and charged toward the nearest man before wheeling around to follow the buckboard. The man grabbed what leather he could find as his horse shied into the next one. That one bucked and kicked out, and in an instant there was a spinning chaos of horses lunging and making stiff-legged leaps. Backward-facing riders gripped onto their cantles with white knuckles, many of them losing their hold and falling among the hoofs and flying dirt. One by one they struggled out of the mêlée and congregated near the muddy riverbank. For members of a religious settlement they knew quite a variety of profanities.

Meanwhile, Kyle followed Luned—and the hog-tied bishop—along the road that pointed the way back to the Keystone Ranch. A day or two would bring them into familiar territory, and in less than a week they might be there. He kept an eye on the back trail, just in case, but no one came riding after them. Two hours passed, then three, and the rhythm of travel cast a sense of relaxation over them. The bishop lay back against the pile of supplies and bedding, muttering to himself but resigned to his fate.

Kyle rode apart, the reins lying easy in his hand. The brim of his hat was level with the horizon. Thompson's plan had worked out perfectly. They had food, horses, bedding, and weapons, and all they had to do now was to cover maybe a hundred miles of open country, and they'd be home.

Chapter Eleven

THE UNEXPECTED GUN

Three years of dry range and deep winters had culled the cattle industry. Big landowners suddenly found themselves poor. Up-and-coming merchants saw their lists of accounts receivable growing daily until they had to close up shop. At the very bottom of the livestock depression were the social misfits, the men of big talk and little character. They had trouble keeping a job in the best of times, and, as herds dwindled and money became tight, they were cut out and sent away carrying nothing but their wages, a bedroll, and an old revolver. The lucky ones were sometimes given a horse from the green string; the rest just hoisted their saddles to their shoulders and began walking. Some gravitated toward California or Oregon. Others took faint and wandering trails back to what they thought of as home, to small worn-out farms in Missouri, Virginia, Tennessee, and Kentucky.

Some of these out-of-work transients carried a grudge against society. They felt that they had been robbed and cheated of their rights, and so they decided they had ample justification for stealing—"foraging", they called it—and made up their minds to take back what they were owed. So they descended from being mediocre hired hands to becoming sneaking chicken thieves. From there some of them went on to try a little highway robbery.

Three of these came across a lonely stretch of stage road and decided to conceal themselves in some rocks and wait for the first easy prey to come along. They would settle for anything. A better horse. A few dollars. Some food.

Kyle and Luned had struck this road around noon on the second day after leaving the compound of schismatic Mormons. The wheel ruts were full of deep silt and made the buckboard ride much more smoothly, and, when Kyle untied the bishop and took the rope from his neck, the chubby man lay back on the pile of bedding and slept while Luned drove. She was so slender and sat so upright on the seat, her light-colored shawl covering her head and shoulders from the sun, that she seemed more spirit than woman.

She and Kyle did not speak except when they stopped for water or had to consider whether to take a side road. Kyle mostly stayed off by himself, alone with his thoughts, the rich hot sun, and the feel of a good horse going at a steady walk.

He looked ahead and saw the road rising into a pair of low hills on which a few trees were struggling to stay alive. He considered riding wide and going around these hills while Luned drove through them, but as they got closer a long dark shadow appeared on the plain, gradually stretching far out from the hills. An arroyo. If he left the road and went around the hills, he would have to cross it somehow. It would be best to stick with the road, so Kyle slowed his horse to a plodding gait and fell in behind the buckboard.

The three desperados, lacking both patience and leadership, jumped the gun by suddenly dashing out into the road as soon as the buggy came within pistol range, waving their arms and calling for the woman to stop. Kyle saw the three as soon as Luned did, and his Colt was in his hand before he thought of reaching for it, but Luned jerked the team off the road right in front of him and his shot went wild. The bishop woke with a startled scream and hung on for dear life as Luned took the buckboard lurching and bouncing through the brush toward the arroyo, the only cover she could see. Her surprise move forced Kyle to make a decision. Should he charge the three men while they were out in the open, or should he stick with Luned and the bishop? There could be more bandits hiding in the arroyo and she'd run right into them. With a curse on his lips, Kyle knew he would stick with the buckboard.

Down in the arroyo, they took shelter under the highest part of a sheer wall. Kyle ordered Luned and Arbeit under the buckboard and gave her the shotgun and extra shells.

"Wait," he said sternly. "Don't shoot until you've got a big enough target so's you don't miss."

He dismounted and crept farther up the draw. It was a poor place to be in. A man could sneak around behind and pin them down while his partner stayed up on the rim and sniped away until he hit one of the horses. Or one of them. Kyle saw a movement, a man sneaking down the hill through the sage. He cocked the Colt and aimed at the opening in the sage where he figured the man would show up next.

Blam!

At least *that* one would stay out of range a while. But where were the other two? Kyle didn't even know how many men had been waiting by those trees. He'd seen three, but there could be more.

Crack!

A shot came zinging over the edge of the arroyo, scattering dirt and narrowly missing the horse. Kyle saw the smoke of the rifle and fired back.

Blam!

While the rifleman kept Kyle's attention, another of the misfits came sneaking up close enough to get a look at the buckboard, then scurried back into the sagebrush to report to his cronies. The one with the rifle kept his eyes on the edge of the arroyo while he listened. The other was counting his cartridges.

"Might not have enough shells f'r a long stand-off," he observed.

"Be worth it!" The scout grinned. "They's a big load of somethin' under a tarp on thet wagon. And a woman!"

"Ah thought thet was a woman drivin'," the third one said.

"Yeah. Not bad, neither. Skinny. She got her a shotgun. Other fella's lyin' under the wagon. I don't think he's got no gun. I shore wanna get t' that woman, boy."

"That other 'un, he's the problem."

"Tell y' what. I'll Injun around thataway"—the one with the rifle pointed the direction—"an' you an' Morgan kinda spread out and crawl up on him. Git 'im in a three-way. One of us'll get him, sure."

"First one t' put a bullet in 'im gets first crack at the woman," Morgan said.

"We'll see which 'un she prefers." The rifleman laughed.

"Let's eat before we do 'er," the third one added. "She kin cook up somethin' outta that pile of stuff, I bet."

"Allus thinkin' of yore belly first," Morgan observed. "All right, let's spread us out an' get this *hombre.*"

To Kyle, things seemed too quiet. He went to the buckboard to tell Luned and Bishop Arbeit to stay put and keep an eye open, and then he went back up the arroyo. Walking along the narrow draw like that, gun in hand and black hat shading his eye, he felt the deeply buried sensations he had known when he was guardian of the ditch. It was almost the same, except that something was missing. He had realized some months ago, at the blacksmith's camp, that he no longer seemed to have the habit of wiping a finger inside his eye patch whenever he was about to do something cold-blooded. But that wasn't it. He was missing some kind of edge. Some of the old quickness to kill just wasn't there.

As if to test this feeling, there was a rustling noise on the rim of the draw and Kyle whirled in time to see a figure rise out of the brush with a rifle. The misfit had the drop on him, but before he could pull the trigger there was a shout. Somebody else, somebody out in the sage, had yelled.

"Hey there!"

"Hah?" The misfit began to look around, following a foolish impulse to see who was talking to him.

Boom!!

Kyle saw him turn toward the voice, then saw him fly off the edge of the draw, hat going one way and rifle the other, to the booming echo of a big rifle going off. Kyle saw the man crash into a crumpled pile almost at his feet, a bloody hole in his chest.

What the . . . ?

The voice came again.

"Hey there!"

Kyle didn't answer. But he holstered the Colt and dove on the rifle, ending up crouched down against the wall of the draw with it. He checked the chamber. At least one round left.

"Hey there! You with the red bandanna!"

From where he was, Kyle could see another man on the other side of the arroyo. This man, wearing a red bandanna, also stood up and exposed himself to see who was calling to him. *Just like an antelope,* Kyle thought. *The way they stand still to watch while some hunter waves a white cloth back and forth, instead of running for their lives.*

"Over here!"

Somewhere above and behind him, the man with the big rifle was making himself known. The second misfit tentatively raised his revolver and, ignoring Kyle altogether, aimed off across the arroyo.

Boom!!

His arms flew in the air, and he stepped back a few paces. Then he dropped like a poll-axed ox.

Kyle knew the next shot could be for him. But at least he could shift position, maybe throw the shooter off a little. He crouched and ran toward the buckboard and saw the third gunman moving up the draw toward them.

"Damn," Kyle said half aloud. *One in front, one in back.*

Luned was no use. She would have to get out from under the buckboard and then get in front of the team to get a clear shot. The team and buckboard were also in Kyle's line of fire, and his run had left him panting and shaky. His aim was not going to be steady. Still, he'd better get off a shot before the misfit got any closer.

Kyle stopped and raised the rifle, but before his thumb had drawn the hammer to full cock, the bigger gun spoke again.

Boom!!

Luned twisted her head to look at Kyle, thinking he had fired the shot, but Kyle was also looking backward. On the rim of the arroyo stood Emil in black coat and black hat, a grim smile on his face and a Winchester .45-90 in his hands.

With a short shovel from under the buckboard seat, Kyle and Emil and the bishop took turns digging the graves. The three dead men had at last laid claim to their own piece of land in the West. Bishop Arbeit borrowed Kyle's book of scripture and said some holy-sounding words over the fresh mounds, and then excused himself to walk a distance down in the arroyo for "nature's call." Luned got the horses turned around and snapped the lines across their backs until they scrambled back up the steep slope and to the road.

"I owe you," Kyle said to Emil when they were alone.

"Not really. I'd been foolin' myself, thinkin' I was goin' t' be a gospel-shoutin' farmer. When y' rode into our compound like y' did, y' made me remember how much I didn't belong there. You were the one what saved me, y' might say."

"Care to ride with us?" Kyle offered.

"I got a horse and pack animal back there a ways," Emil said. "Might catch up with y', might not. Rather stay alone for a while. But I imagine I'll be 'round somewhere, if y' look."

"Fair enough," Kyle said. "We're headin' for the Keystone Ranch, north of here. You'd be welcome." They shook hands, and Kyle watched the man in the black coat ride away.

Going to find the bishop, Kyle found the spot where the man had watered the sand. He also found footprints leading away, down the draw, footprints spaced far apart like a man in a hurry. Arbeit was hurrying south. *Let him go,* Kyle thought. *Have to turn him loose sooner or later, anyway. Good riddance, if anything.*

Sundown found Kyle and Luned looking toward a low building on the horizon ahead of them. They saw the silhouette of a windmill and corrals and what looked to be a pole barn.

"A stage stop, I s'pose," Kyle said.

"But who stops there?" Luned asked. "We haven't seen anyone all day, except those outlaws. Not a stagecoach, not a wagon, not even a rider. I'm beginning to think this road is abandoned."

"Could happen. In Colorado, one time, I followed a good road right into a burned-out stage station. Seems the company found a quicker cut-off for the coaches."

"At least there would be water, wouldn't there? Perhaps some shelter for the horses, in case it storms."

Kyle looked at the sky, twisting in the saddle so his one good eye could see the entire horizon. In every direction the sky was endlessly clear, light blue up above, steel gray where it touched the earth.

"Storms?" he said. "Not hardly."

Still, it was a place. It turned out to be inhabited. Luned turned the team in through the leaning gateposts and pulled up in front of the sagging log structure. Low and mean, it was built of mismatched crooked logs, chinking falling out in big pieces. A bit of light showed through the chinks and glowed behind the dirty window. Smoke came from the chimney. Two underfed horses stood in the corral, heads drooping. Kyle remained in the saddle, and Luned made no move to climb down from the buckboard. It was quiet in the twilight except when the team blew and stamped, jingling their harness.

Finally the latch was lifted from within, and the plank door swung open on leather hinges. A man in coveralls and undershirt stooped to exit the low doorway. A smell followed him, the odor of sweat and dead meat and smoldering cottonwood.

"Light down," he said. "Water trough's yonder. Jus' filled it this afternoon."

Kyle watered the horses but didn't unhitch or unsaddle. Luned washed her face and hands at a basin sitting on a crude plank behind the building. The back door opened. A burly, sour woman came out with a chamber pot. She carried it into the sage and emptied it, and on her way back to the building she noticed Luned at the basin.

"Got no hot water," she snapped. "Didn't know anybody was comin'."

Luned rejoined Kyle, and the man waved them toward the low doorway. "Got supper an' a room. Half a dollar apiece."

Inside was the familiar lay-out of a stagecoach stop. There was one big room with cook stove and fireplace and a long plank table. One lamp with a dirty chimney hung over the table, giving off a feeble yellow light, and another one stood on a pie safe next to the back door. At the table there were enough benches and stools for eight or ten people. An L on the back of the building provided sleeping quarters for the stationkeepers, and there were two small rooms for passengers.

"Only got one room," the husky woman growled, lighting a candle from the lamp and taking it into the corner room. "Boy sleeps in t'other."

She returned to the main room where she set about stirring her stew.

As his eye became accustomed to the gloom, Kyle saw the "supper" he and Luned had interrupted. It consisted of a shapeless mound of salt pork and a chunk of bread sitting on the bare table and three bowls of what looked like greasy stew.

Luned looked into the bedroom and drew back. It was small, dark, and musty, and the furniture consisted of a wooden chair and a narrow bed. The blankets were stained.

She looked at Kyle and made a small no movement with her head.

"Reckon we'll go on a ways," Kyle said, gesturing for Luned to get outside while he eased backward and kept his eye on the man and woman. "Thanks for the water."

The man snarled, and the woman reached her hand behind her.

"Got no money, huh?" the man said.

"Let's just say we're used to sleepin' in the open," Kyle said. Luned had made it out. Now all he had to do was get out without turning his back on these two.

The woman's blank-faced expression didn't change, but she was cautiously sidling toward the back door. The man was smiling through broken yellow teeth and had one hand behind his back. Watching them, Kyle remembered the cave and how it felt to feel threatened in such a dark place. He could smell the fear, could smell the tense air. His gun hand began to itch, and he tried to think whether he had slipped his holster's hammer loop off the hammer. His elbow touched the edge of the open door.

Outside, there was a sudden scream and a hoarse, hard laugh. Then another scream.

Luned!

Kyle recalled the words of the woman—"Boy sleeps in t'other." There was a third person here, some over-grown lout they called "Boy". He must have been outside and grabbed Luned as soon as she stepped out. Kyle turned, crouching and making his draw at the same time. But it was a mistake to turn his back on the couple, and it was nearly his last mistake. Realizing it, he whirled in time to see the woman bringing up a shotgun that must have been standing next to the back door. She was fumbling, trying to cock the hammers.

The man had his own gun. The hand that had been behind his back now had a short-barrel Colt in it, and he fired from the hip.

Whoom!

In the low room the shot sounded like a cannon, and the concussion put the lamps out. Sudden and total darkness. Kyle's instinct was to get out, but he knew that the woman with the shotgun could see him outlined in the doorway. He dodged to the side just as the first blast ripped past him. He fired into the dark, aiming at her muzzle flash, and, after the roaring in his ears died down, he heard her groaning.

166

There was a sound off to his left like the man had stumbled against one of the benches. Kyle held his breath and blinked his good eye, trying to see through the gunsmoke in the dark. As his eye became adjusted, a window slowly appeared as a dim rectangle in the far wall and the long table became a darker part of the shadows. Then he saw what he had been waiting for. A movement, just a part of the darkness moving.

Kyle's Colt spoke again, and in the muzzle flash he saw the evil face and the yellow teeth screaming, and then there was darkness again and silence.

Kyle jumped for the doorway and dove under the buckboard where he could reload and scan the skyline for signs of Luned and her captor. From ground level he could see the silhouette of his own horse, the water trough, the brush lining the far side of the stage road, hills far in the distance, but no movement. And the night was as quiet as a tomb.

Kyle flipped open the Colt's loading gate and reloaded by feel. Then he crawled out and stood up.

"Damn."

He untied his horse and swung into the saddle, half expecting a shot to come out of the dark sage once he was outlined against the sky. On the horizon, a half moon was just emerging.

Kyle scanned and listened, scanned and listened, and soon he got a feeling that the ambusher had taken Luned across the road and off into the sage. Each time he turned in that direction, he could sense her presence. He moved the horse that way, going slow, leaning forward to see into the dark.

Then he saw the gleam, faint and distant. Just a spot of white with weak moonlight hitting it, almost like a piece of paper dangling from a bush. Kyle lowered himself along the horse's neck so his silhouette would blend with the animal's and rode forward. Cautiously.

He expected a shot, and it came. The *boom* of a big rifle came like a breeze over the tops of the sagebrush. Kyle strained to see. The boom was followed by another one as he kicked the horse into a run toward the sound. Nobody was shooting at him, but somebody was shooting. Kyle was less than a quarter mile from the buildings when he saw the pale figure walking toward him.

Luned. And she was carrying a pistol. He could see the shine of it against her light-colored dress.

He reined up when he reached her. She handed up the gun, stepped into the stirrup he cleared for her, and pulled herself up behind him to hold him around the waist with her head against his back. She was breathing hard and trembling, and she was cold.

"What happened?"

"He must have been out there at the buckboard, going through my things. I walked right into him, and he grabbed me."

"I heard you scream," Kyle said.

"It was awful. That huge filthy hand over my face. And all the time he dragged me with him, he kept hissing in my ear. I can't even repeat the things he said. The way he talked! Things he would do to me. How he would kill you if the other two didn't. I heard the shooting, and he said they'd killed you. But then he heard the horse coming."

"So how did you get hold of his gun?" Kyle asked.

"I didn't. He had one hand over my face and kept dragging me backward, and he had his gun out. Before I knew it, two shots came from somewhere and he fell down with a bloody hole in his chest and blood pouring out. I didn't think, I just grabbed up the gun and ran back this way."

"You suppose he's still alive out there?" Kyle said.

Near them and coming out of the dark, a third voice spoke quietly.

"No chance of that," the voice said.

"Emil!" Luned said.

"Again," Kyle said.

"I'm thinking you two need a guardian," Emil said.

When the sun was up and they were out of sight of the stage station, Kyle built a good fire, and, from her stock of supplies, Luned fixed them a breakfast of flapjacks and side meat. She apologized for not having coffee, but the Mormons prohibited the poisonous stuff in their compound, along with alcohol. Emil rode back to the station and returned with coffee and a sack of canned goods and flour.

"You stole that," Kyle said with a grin.

"Probably they stole it first," Emil said.

As they ate, Emil went on talking.

"I saw you stop at the station," he said, "but I also saw there wasn't any stage teams anywhere in sight. So I thought I'd scout the place before I came in. Found their hide-out hole, half mile over that way. That's where that half-wit was headed with Luned. Not far from it, there's a half dozen recent graves. None too deep, neither. A couple o' wolves had one of 'em dug up and was gnawin' on 'im. Those killers must have murdered quite a few people in their sleep. Right in that same bedroom."

Luned shuddered.

"Guess we need to take care of the bodies," Kyle said.

"You two go on ahead. I'll do it."

"That's a lot of diggin'," Kyle said.

"I think I'll just put all three of 'em in that dug-out cellar, and set fire to it. Kind of a cremation. Better than they deserve. I'd let the wolves have 'em, except that I kinda like wolves."

Chapter Twelve

THREE TO THE KEYSTONE

Gwen stood on the broad front porch and pouted. All these glorious summer days and no one with whom to share them. Art was always off on business, managing a Keystone Ranch three times the size of the original. The hard times forced more and more small ranchers to give up, selling Art their places for a fraction of their value. Gwen enjoyed planning the new additions to the house and watching the builders at work, but now it was finished and furnished and sometimes—not always, but sometimes—all it provided was more space in which to be bored.

Link was never around, since he had to do more of Art's work. He used to stop by the house, occasionally, to ask her to ride with him out to inventory some livestock or check on operations at one of the outlying ranches, but he was too busy now.

She had written to Julia, inviting her to bring her new husband for a long visit, but the newlyweds went to Europe instead. She had Fontana to talk to, of course, but Gwen found her too serious these days, ever since they had word of Luned's being held by the black coat colony. Fontana played the piano, but preferred slow and gloomy works. It was almost as if she had lost the spirit of life.

Gwen and Fontana went for walks in the early morning or late evening to avoid the scorching sun, but even then Fontana was generally more pessimistic than necessary. If Gwen pointed out a newly opened flower with a drop of dew balanced on one petal, Fontana would say: "The poor thing, to be all dried and wilted by noon." When Gwen remarked on the evening breeze being refreshing, Fontana would complain that it dried her skin to shoe leather. When Gwen suggested they take a buggy and food and blankets and spend two or three days in the cool mountains, Fontana would decline, saying she preferred not to sleep on hard ground. That campfire smoke irritated her eyes.

The two of them took trips to town whenever Art could spare a man or two to go along as protection against the riff-raff that infested the dried-up rangeland. But even in town Fontana was somber. She imagined each merchant was waiting to cheat them. She believed the hotel overcharged them for rooms and meals. She often fell into vague distraction as she studied the faces of strangers, gazing at tall men in particular.

Gwen did not complain, at least not openly. She did appreciate having another woman for company. She, Fontana, and Mary, the cook, spent many afternoons putting up preserves and cooking, and she and Fontana could sit together for hours doing embroidery or playing cards. It was just that with Art or with Link or with Julia there were afternoons and evenings of fun and laughter. Even stodgy old Art was more fun to walk with than Fontana. When she pointed out a new flower to Art, or teased him into taking a few days— and nights!—in the mountains, he would laugh with those loving little crinkles at the corners of his eyes. He loved it when she discovered joy in little, daily things. One day he reminded her of an autumn week they had spent riding in the mountains, looking at the changing colors of the aspen, and Gwen promised herself she would get everything ready for another camping trip, just the two of them, up among the golden and yellow groves. She would get everything ready and surprise him by dragging him away from his work.

Well, she thought, *when summer is over and the cattle have been rounded up and sold, then maybe he'll have more time to spend at home. Maybe,* she thought, *we'll take that trip to St. Louis he's been promising me forever.* She spent hours with her illustrated book, THE WONDERS OF ST. LOUIS, and her stereopticon pictures of the city's gardens and studied her catalogs of dress patterns.

Meanwhile, far south of the Keystone, a slender woman in white and a tall cowboy with an eye patch traveled northward, parallel with the mountain range. Sometimes they followed two-track roads, leading east, in order to avoid regions of deep gullies and high hills. Sometimes they struck north across untracked prairie. Kyle often rode ahead, almost out of sight of the buckboard. He said he was scouting the way for the wagon, but in truth he wanted to be alone with quiet sounds like the breeze in the grass and the horse's hoofs on the earth.

Once he discovered a broad stream of clear water meandering through low hills, forming deep pools where it eddied against its corners. He rode back and led Luned to a wide shallow stretch where she could water the team, then went a mile upstream to water his own horse and take a plunge. The water was too clear, too cool to resist. He stripped the horse and then stripped himself down to his white skin and took the horse into the deepest eddy he could find. He scrubbed the horse with his hands and dunked himself over and over. Clean and shivering, he finally pulled himself up onto the wet horse and rode bareback and naked up onto the bank. There he rubbed the animal with handfuls of fresh grass.

Kyle paused and leaned with his elbows across the horse's back, looking off across the wide plain. So much sunlight. Such a sky. He remembered being a dirty, stinking creature in a burrow, and he recalled the suffocating smoke of a smudgy fire in the darkness. He thought of the blizzard wind bearing down on him. And now, in all this sun-hot prairie, it seemed only a story about someone he never knew, in a time before he was born.

When he was dry, Kyle dressed himself and saddled the horse and rode up out of the stream bed to rejoin Luned.

She, too, had given in to the temptation of cool running water. He rode up onto a hill above the shallow oxbow where he had left her and saw the wagon standing up to its wheel hubs in the stream, the horses placidly cooling their legs and standing motionless as if asleep with the pleasure of it. Upstream of the wagon, Luned was floating on her back with one hand holding to a bunch of grass to keep from drifting down the current. Her white dress floated all around her like someone had spread a disk of lace on the water and placed her on it. Or like a white swan had fallen into the stream with its wings spreading wide across the surface.

From where he sat, Kyle could see how Luned's hair flowed over the bosom of her dress and how the dress moved languidly up and down with the current. Except for the fact that her eyes were closed and her lips pressed tightly together, she could have been the banshee at rest in a world turned upside down by some magic so that the reflecting surface of the stream became the sky and she became a white cloud in the shape of a woman.

Kyle whistled so she would know he was there. He rode down to the edge of the water, and the buckboard team looked around at him.

At first, Luned did not move, and Kyle had the strange sudden thought that she might be dead. But then with a sigh, she released her hold on the grass and let her feet sink down to find the bottom. She rose from the water and waded toward the tailboard of the wagon with her skirts flowing ahead of her on the current.

She sat down and pressed the water from her skirts, pulled the water from her hair, and smoothed it down across her back to dry. Her boots and stockings were on the seat of the buckboard, but when she made her way over the luggage and bedding to take up the reins, she put them in the bed of the wagon and remained barefooted. She sat and spread out her skirts on the wide seat and clucked the team into movement again.

They traveled together for an hour.

"Back there with all that clear water," Kyle finally said, "I got to thinkin' about the ditch." He did not look at her, but kept his eyes on the distant horizon.

"The Great North project," she said. "Yes. The water. So clear."

"Cold, that water."

"Yes."

"I used t' ride along the ditch, lookin' at it," Kyle said, "but I don't recall ever bein' tempted to get in it."

"It was very pure, that water, very clear," Luned said. Her voice was distant and small as if her mind had gone back to those faraway mountains. "It was Fontana's, that water. That is why. That is why you would not swim in it. She controlled it. She controlled everything about the project . . . the workers, the families, the plans to irrigate all the land under the mountains. Even you. You remember."

"Yeah," Kyle said to the horizon. "I guess I do. I used to ride clear up to the highest gate on that ditch sometimes, tryin' to get away from that feeling. From her."

"But you couldn't," Luned said. "She was the ditch. Everything the water touched was under her will. Even when you killed her Guardian . . . you remember . . . even then you could not leave. Could you? Neither could I, or the hermit who built the gates and knew how to make them work. Each of us could do something she could not do, yet we could not leave her. Not until the water was taken."

She stopped the team, and he held the horses while she stepped into the back of the wagon and opened her bedroll. When she took her seat again, she had the quirt in her hand.

"This does not need to be between us," she said. "Not any longer. Take it."

Kyle took it and looked at the ring woven into the braid.

"Thank you," was all he could think of to say.

They came to a fence out in the middle of nowhere. Kyle could see that it ran west at least another mile, so he turned east and scouted along it until he found a gate. A gate, and a road, that would take them north.

Kyle fell silent and studied the ground intently. Fresh tracks on the road showed that a single rider had passed along it recently. After a time, the tracks turned off into the brush. He wanted to follow them, but decided he'd better stay with Luned.

"I was wondering," he said, turning back to look at her. But his words were cut short by what he saw.

Luned had risen on her feet and was standing on the bouncy seat of the buckboard, still holding the reins. She stood with her bare feet well spread for balance, holding the leather lines very casually. Kyle thought of a picture he once saw of a woman in a circus show, riding, standing up on two horses. He thought again of the banshee, the white dress and the pale hair floating behind her on the breeze.

"What were you wondering?" Luned asked in that voice of distant fragility.

Kyle recovered himself. He couldn't think why seeing her that way had startled him so. She was only doing it so her dress would dry faster.

"Ah," he said, "I was thinking how you used the word *was* back there. About Fontana. You saying she isn't there now? I know about the black coats taking over the project and all. But where is she? Do you know?"

Luned stepped down to stand in front of the seat, still holding the lines lightly.

"Those intruders ruined it all. More than just taking the water for themselves. I tried to stop them. You had gone away. I tried, but I was not enough. Our workmen would not fight men with guns. They had been living on promises for too many years, seeing their families do without. Some slipped away in the night, and it was said they went to the gold camps to become rich. Some of the weak ones joined the black coat men. For Fontana, all was finished."

"So Fontana . . ."—Kyle searched for words—"she's . . . ?"

"Dead?" Luned said softly. "No."

"You've seen her? Don't tell me that ol' what's-his-name, Arbeit, that he's keepin' her some place. . . ."

"No. I have not seen her. She was so angry with you. I was angry as well, and rode to the Keystone to find you. The black coat men chased after me. I have not seen her since. But she is at the Keystone with your friends. We will find her waiting for us."

"Just like that," Kyle said. "How could you know that?"

"Don't sneer," Luned said to him. "You still don't know who I am. But I will tell you this . . . we both need her.

Once, long ago, I lived where all was darkness, where each day brought the face of death and never came the sun. Buried like a dried-up seed and waiting for something to bring me back to life. Whether you believe it or not, Kyle Owen, we both live because of her. You and I."

Kyle turned to study her, and saw that she was looking ahead at something in the road. He shifted his gaze and saw a horse and rider in dark clothes, a sudden materialization, blocking the way. He had something draped across the saddle in front of him—something the size of a human.

They urged the horses forward and discovered Emil, smiling, waiting for them, a freshly dressed deer across the saddle. He dropped it into the bed of the buckboard.

"Fresh meat," he said.

"Thought I heard a shot, a while ago," Kyle spoke the words, but his thoughts stayed with what Luned had said.

"Must've been me," Emil said. "I was goin' up the road and saw this little buck on top of a ridge. Figured we oughta have one good cook-up of venison before the trip's over with."

"Over with?" Kyle repeated, his thoughts being jerked back to the present. Luned was not surprised at the expression. She seemed to expect it.

"Got to that hill over there," Emil said, pointing with his rifle to indicate a high and faraway rise in the prairie, almost a mesa. "Y' can see a long ways there. The road comes t' a river, 'nother road, some fence. So I rode on down there."

"And found what?" Kyle asked.

Luned was already looking through the hill and across the miles of river and road. "He found what you are seeking," she said. "Emil has seen the Keystone. You are nearly home."

"It's Keystone range, all right," Emil said. "Where the road crosses a bridge there's a Keystone boundary marker."

"Nearly home," Kyle repeated. The word felt foreign in his mouth. Nowhere had been home to him since he was a boy.

"Yes," Luned said. "It seems you are."

Kyle turned and looked down the back trail, his face shaded by the level-set Stetson. Again he remembered the freezing huddled remnant of a man living in a dry, dark burrow. Again he remembered the blacksmith with his wagons and forge far from anyone who needed a smith. There came a memory of the way they had used fire and earth to break open the ditch and set the water free. The way the water had flooded the Mormon fields. It had all been like a dream of chaos in which he and the blacksmith hovered above the black coats like two figures carrying death and destruction.

Kyle turned back and took his place beside the buckboard, and the three of them rode forward together. Two strong tall men, well mounted, between them a woman as light and insubstantial as a spirit, a fantasy of cloud and mist pale with wild hair, driving a team and wagon.

Kyle wanted to camp on Keystone land that night, and so they drove over the bridge and continued on until they came to a small grove by a clear stream. Luned approved of the camp site because the stream showed no trace of cattle, no piles of manure on the grass, no deep hoof holes in the mud, no ruined banks.

Luned put on her boots and vanished among the upstream willows. Kyle and Emil made a fire pit and rigged a lean-to out of the wagon tarp, then watered the horses and put them on a picket line and gathered up firewood. Emil hung his deer to a tree branch to skin it and cut out steaks for supper.

Kyle hunkered down to stir the fire, and he looked around at all the country—the long plains sloping away to the east, the low swells of hills north and south, the darkening shadow mountains to the west. He was at peace here. From the moment they drove past the Keystone boundary marker, he had felt close to the center of things again. Not far from here, and, very soon, he would be back among the men he knew, men with whom he now felt a bond stronger than steel welded at a forge.

He breathed deeply, drawing in the air as if, by inhaling, he could capture and hold the circle of light enclosing him on all sides with safety and certainty. Here on this range, dry as it was and devoid of cattle, he was at home.

"Better throw up some more dirt for a windscreen 'round that fire," Emil observed. "Th' grass around here's like tinder. She'd go with a spark."

Emil got two wagon rods from the buckboard and put them over the coals to hold the sizzling venison steaks. Kyle scouted the meadow to find wild Indian potatoes, what some people called breadroot. Several of them he coated with clay mud and set in the coals to bake. He sliced up the others and put them to boil. When Luned returned, she started a pot of coffee and set the pot of beans on the fire. The men dragged a fallen cottonwood log over to the fire to sit on.

They ate. They talked, a little. The sun went down behind the far mountains. The air began to cool, and, as the prairie night came crawling over them, they let the fire die. Luned went to lie down in the lean-to, a ghostly white figure in the dark shadow. Emil and Kyle rolled out blankets by the fire pit. Kyle lay on his back, looking up into the immensity of stars, his hair ruffled by a breeze that may have just that moment arrived after crossing a thousand miles of open plain, free and clean and alive. If he dreamed that night, his dreams troubled him not at all.

In the morning they rode out of the stream valley. The silhouette of the distant mountain range had the dull bluish-green color of old copper, and looked familiar. The grass was dry, and cattle were few. And then, passing through a swale in the hills, they saw that the range had burned. The blackened area stretched from the far fence all the way over the adjoining hill. What once was grass had become powdered char. Cow chips and sage bushes were piles of white ash.

"Grass fire," Kyle said. "Bad stuff."

"I wonder what started it?" Luned said. "Lightning?"

"Yeah, lightning can do it. Or some waddie tossing a cigarette butt. Or wind hittin' a campfire."

The scorched area became narrower as they rode along, and at a gate in the barbed wire fence it suddenly stopped. It was clear to see that the fire had started there and spread as it went downwind. It was pretty easy to see what had started it. There was a circle of rocks, and inside the circle was a metal bar and deep, powdery ash. Somebody had thrown together a hasty fire pit so they could heat that bar. And they had started to make it into a circle, a loop.

"Here's why," Emil said. He was studying the way the gate was fastened shut with twisted barbed wire.

"Gate loop?" Kyle said.

"Yeah. Some fence rider with nuthin' better to do. I'll bet he found that old rod there and figured he'd make a nice gate loop out of it. These here barb-wire loops tear up a man's gloves sumthin' awful."

"And the fire got away from him."

"Looks like."

They passed the gate and traveled on together, the two horsemen flanking the buckboard.

Kyle pointed to a mountain and said its name. "They call it Beaverhead. Looks like one, I guess."

An hour later and he knew the name of the creek they crossed.

"This would be Young's Creek. They say a man named Young found gold in it, but I doubt it."

When the road joined a wider one, more traveled, he said he had ridden that road before. "This leads off southeast . . . that direction there . . . and comes to the old stage road, 'way out there. The way we're goin', it takes us right past the Keystone front gate."

They came over a low rise and into a wetter valley where there was green grass and groves of chokecherry and plum and willow. Three prairie chickens flew up from the side of the road.

"You go on ahead," Emil said, untying the shotgun from his slicker behind the cantle. "I think I'll try to shoot some of those prairie chickens for supper. It's only neighborly, comin' into a place, to bring somethin' for the pot."

Luned and Kyle went on. They found little to talk about as they rode on into the Keystone, the summer afternoon arching over the range and over the mountains with comfortable heat. Now and then a jack rabbit started from the brush near the road. A rattlesnake slithered across in front of the team. Unseen birds piped short bursts of melody out in the sage. Somewhere a maverick calf bawled for its mother. The day was singing and moving with life all around them. Kyle felt he was free from wanting to hide away in the darkness of a cave, eager to return to an unfinished life, to close the gates he had opened.

Some men, moving steers, waved to them, and they waved back. A rider coming along the road lifted his hand in greeting and said it was a nice day; Luned smiled and Kyle nodded, for neither of them knew the man.

When the roofline of Art Pendragon's house appeared on the horizon, Kyle's feeling of being home turned into feelings of anxious hesitation. He reined in the horse, and Luned stopped the team. Both sat looking ahead, not at each other.

"If Fontana is there," Luned said, "what will you say?"

"I was just wonderin' that myself. I don't know."

The last years flooded his mind, the images of darkness, the suffocating stench of smoke in the cave, the knife-keen wind of the cañon, the howling face. The crouching and hiding, the killing, the terror of the sounds coming through the earth. How was he going to tell anyone about it, especially her? But she, or someone, would eventually ask where he had spent those years, and he would have to have an answer, an answer they would understand.

Luned suddenly spoke, startling him out of his thoughts.

"It is all in the past," she said.

"What?" Kyle turned his head and found her looking directly at him. He could not look away. The pale eyes gazed into his face until all dark thoughts faded back and back, and then were gone from his head. Instead, slowly, there grew in his head the idea that he should ride over to the shade of the cottonwoods on their right and stay there while Luned drove on into the ranch yard. He looked into her eyes, calm and knowing, and understood her meaning. She *would* go ahead of him. Kyle suddenly remembered the day he had ridden into Crannog and a little boy had come running to open the corral gate for him. Luned would tell the story, where they had been, and the way would be open for him.

Without a word he nodded and rode to the cottonwoods. From there he could see the house, the fences, the barns, and stables. He dismounted and drank in the sight of it all. The place seemed so clean, so ordered, so strong. He took his canteen from the saddle and raised it in a salute to the Keystone before drinking deeply.

Years after, looking back on the warm summer day with the Keystone buildings spread out below him, Kyle would remember it as a strange experience, the way Luned had driven off. In his memory was etched how, when she drove the buckboard away, he could hear the jingle of the harness and the squeaks of the wagon all the way to the house, but he knew it was not possible. And there was the dust. The road was dusty, and his horse's hoofs raised little clouds at each step, yet the buckboard's wheels seemed to raise no dust at all.

A man sitting and peeling potatoes in the shade at the side of the house saw the wagon coming and limped inside. Kyle recognized the limp. It was Pat, Mary's husband. The large woman herself came bustling out, wiping her hands on her apron, then Art and Gwen came out the front door, Gwen shading her eyes with her hand.

The buckboard stopped, Luned got down and went up the steps to the porch, and one more figure came out the door. Darkly clothed, her posture erect and dignified even at this distance, Kyle knew it was Fontana. She was there.

He stood watching even after the six figures went back into the house. He was not impatient, and he was not anxious. He heard the horse cropping grass, heard a little clatter of breeze in the cottonwood leaves, and the far-off ring of a hammer on an anvil, and he was content with the moment he was in.

Finally she came out onto the porch and shielded her eyes with her hand to search along the windbreak of high cottonwoods until she saw him in the shadows, a tall figure wearing his Stetson straight and level.

He saw her descend the stairs gracefully, and she came toward him with the soft dignity he remembered so well. As she drew close, she recognized the black eye patch, and he saw her gathering her brows, slightly, and clenching her lips, lightly, and he knew she was nervous in spite of how calm and deliberate she looked to be. The realization almost took away his nervousness.

She was hatless, and, when she entered the shadows, it was as if her shining hair had caught the sunlight and brought it trailing after her. In her hands she carried a delicate blue beaker of cool water.

Near enough now to touch him, she held out the crystal glass, and he took it and drank deeply, looking into her face.

He returned it, and she drank, also gazing into his face. She gracefully bent at the knees as if she were doing a curtsey and placed the beaker on the grass, then rose again to face him. She did not know what he would say or do. She had not known what to say. But both knew how the water was a symbol between them, how it had many meanings that words could never reach.

Six years since they had seen each other. Her power over him, once irresistible, had drained away like the waters of the broken ditch. As he stood looking at her, his mind saw the face of the banshee; his mind struggled with it, cleared itself of the image, and the animal of the burrow looked out of his one good eye and saw deeply into the woman before him. He heard her breathing, listened to the slight rustle of her dress. For a moment he felt unknown things creeping toward him as they had in the cave, but in the next moment they were silenced.

He knew she was no longer the lady of the water, the indomitable will. He was no longer her murderous Guardian. He knew he was free to brush her away now, if he wished. He was also free to love her.

And so he lifted both arms toward her, and she stepped between them and let him draw her in and hold her. She pressed her face to his chest.

"It's all gone," she said at last. "They took Crannog. The project is gone."

"I know," Kyle said, his lips against her hair.

"I've been here a very long time," she said, "hoping you would come."

"I've been gone a long time," he answered.

As it turned out, it was Luned, rather than Kyle or Fontana, who answered the unasked questions. In the evening, after supper, she would quietly place her napkin beside her plate and glide into the new parlor; sometimes no one saw her go. Art and Gwen and Fontana and Kyle and Emil and Link and any Keystone guests, who happened to be there, would go to the parlor, and there she would be. Art offered brandy or bourbon to the men while Gwen poured light wine or tea for the women, and Luned would begin to speak. One evening she told how they had found the place where the range fire burned the grass. One evening she told the episode at the stage station. Several evenings she related her experiences with the men of the black coats, holding her audience spellbound as she described how they tried to convert her to their religion. And, of course, she narrated, with many smiles and dancing eyes, the story of how Kyle imitated one of the Mormon enforcers and terrified the schismatic leader, Brother Arbeit.

One evening she said that Kyle, too, had been a sort of prisoner . . . of the cañon in which he lived alone. She said it was very fortunate that the blacksmith—they all remembered Mr. Evan Thompson, the smith—had found Kyle when he did. Very fortunate. The odd thing was this: Kyle could not remember telling Luned about it. Perhaps he had, but his memory of the trip north with Luned was very clear, and it did not include telling her about the cave in the cañon or of the strange appearance of the blacksmith far from anyone who needed him.

Luned's evening narratives gave Kyle and Fontana more breathing room, more time to go walking or riding together. Kyle found the Keystone Ranch familiar, yet new in many ways—the new additions to the house, new barns, better fences, new men working there—and there was much about Fontana he found both familiar and yet new.

During his time at Crannog, he had known her as the woman who directed the Great North irrigation project, sitting her sidesaddle like an empress, issuing commands to gangs of workers. He had lived in her house where she held absolute sway over everything that went on. At the Keystone many days would go by before he would see her as she had become, a woman of few expectations, of little power, of no property. Just a woman.

Fontana, too, needed time to get used to Kyle. She had known him as a grim-jawed guardian of ditches and water gates, a man who seemed to be angry with the whole world even while she held him in a mysterious bondage. But now, walking and riding with him at her side, she felt the calmness of the man. No longer was he so independent; indeed, he seemed linked into all the other men on the Keystone. He seemed to be part of the buildings and ranges, part of a very large whole. He waved to men who passed them coming and going from the ranch, spoke easily with Pat and Mary in the kitchen, sometimes lounged in the shade with other cowhands, petting one of the ranch dogs and talking of cattle and weather. He belonged in all this.

Meanwhile, Luned's quiet stories went on. Gwen and Art came to feel they had known Kyle and Luned and Emil for a very long time. She wove her tales with careful words, yet it was not the words the people remembered but the feeling the words caused. After a time it seemed natural that Kyle would have been gone all those years, that Luned's anger with him was understandable. It was too bad about the Great North project, but now there seemed to be a bright future somewhere ahead.

The evening finally came when the stories were done. The same people gathered in the parlor, including a new visitor from England who was interested in Western breeds of cattle. Luned was there, but silent.

Art Pendragon offered drinks, as usual, and opened the carved cigar box on the sideboard as an invitation to any gentleman who cared to smoke. The men were standing in that corner of the room, the corner with the liquor cabinet.

"Emil?" Art said. "Care for a cigar?"

Emil laughed a spontaneous laugh, loud enough for the ladies to look around in surprise.

"Sorry," he said quickly. "I was just comparing your hospitality with Arbeit and his Mormons back there. They might 'a' been jacklegs and dissenters, but they still never allowed tobacco or whisky. Or even coffee. There was times I'd 'a' sold my soul for a tin cup full of Arbuckle's followed by a 'bible' and fixin's!"

The English visitor looked at him strangely.

"Pardon me? Would it be considered rude, I wonder, to ask for translation?"

It was Art's turn to laugh. "Not rude at all," he said. "What Emil said just now means he used t' trail cattle." Seeing that the Englishman was still puzzled, Art continued: "He used to make his living herdin' cattle up the trail from Texas. Which trail was it, Emil?"

"Great Western, mostly. Once on the Goodnight-Loving, but she's pretty much closed off by barb wire and railroads."

"To a trail herder," Art explained, "a 'bible' is a packet of cigarette papers and fixin's, of course, refers to the tobacco. And since most of the coffee carried on the chuck wagons came in bags with the Arbuckle brand name on them, cowboys liked to call it Arbuckle's instead of coffee."

"I see," said the Englishman. "And I can safely add that if your Arbuckle's is anything like this stuff you Americans call whisky, I won't be drinking much of it. But," he addressed Emil with new curiosity, "I suppose you must miss that romantic way of life. The open plains, the camaraderie, and all."

Emil snorted and helped himself to two fingers of bourbon from Art's decanter.

"Not much to miss," he said. "A trail herder spends twelve, fourteen hours in the saddle. You're forever treatin' for screwworms or draggin' dumb heifers outta mud holes. Man breathes so much alkali dust it makes his nose bleed. Sleeps on cactus. Sometimes rides half the day with a dumb stinking calf across the saddle looking for its ma. And as for your camaraderie . . . well, you do meet some awful good men. But then there's those that are runnin' from something, or don't fit in anywhere they go. Some y' can't depend on, and on a trail drive that makes 'em dangerous. No, I don't guess I miss it."

"Quite a speech," Art said.

Conversation drifted from whisky to railroads and hunting before Art brought it back to the cattle business.

"Been hard times for cattle around here," he began. "Lot of ranchers selling off their breeding stock along with the rest of the herd. But I'm thinking the rain will come back, and, if we can keep our breeders and hybrids healthy, we'll stand to make a good profit. Gwen keeps ridin' me for buying up busted-out ranches and leasing so much range, but it lets me keep the herds moving from place to place. That's the trick. Don't let 'em chew the grass down to the bare ground. Move 'em to a new range. Kyle, you might recall those longhorns? They're makin' a comeback again, and I've got a plan in mind to breed 'em with a smaller animal, maybe Hereford. Maybe even those little Scotch cattle."

The English expert sniffed at that. The very image of a huge longhorn bull—nothing less than an ox, really— mounting a small Highland cow was ludicrous. For a Highland bull to mate with a longhorn cow seemed impossible. These Americans!

"Glad you're doing OK," Kyle said. "Came through a whole lot of country without a steer to be seen anywhere."

"Here's my point," Art said. "I could use you and Emil to ramrod my scheme. As is, I'm having to ride out to all points of the compass and stay out there, supervising. Just moving the herd one time sometimes takes me away for a week or more."

Emil turned his head to look at Gwen over his shoulder, her hair shining in the lamplight across the room. "See what you mean." He grinned.

"Yeah," Art said. "So, Link has plenty on his hands these days, and most of my men are good workers but poor organizers."

"It seems like Emil could do that on his own," Kyle said. "Two ramrods have a way of tanglin' up with each other."

"Right. But I'd like it if both of you would take it on, for starters. I got a hunch I'll end up using one of you on another project I got in mind."

"I'm willin', if Kyle is," Emil said.

"Done," Kyle said.

"Good," Art said. "Oh, and I've got just the man to help you. Garth Cochran. In fact, I'm pretty sure he's the fence rider who started that grass fire that Luned told us about. He said he was fixin' a gate and his fire got away from him. But he's OK. Came to the Keystone about the time you left, Kyle."

"Oh, no! You don't mean the one we called the new kid, do you?"

"You got it," Art said. "You two can have him and the longhorns to boot. I'd call that a fair challenge, wouldn't you?"

"Any more whisky in that bottle?" Kyle asked.

Chapter Thirteen

"WAS EVER WOMAN IN THIS MANNER WOO'D?"

King Richard III
William Shakespeare

The days of late summer fell into a comfortable routine for Kyle. Sometimes together and sometimes alone, he and Emil rode to the far corners of the Keystone range in order to move cattle to fresh grass or better water. More often than not, it meant simply sitting on a hill in some shade to watch the cattle graze. Evenings out there dragged into chilly nights, the long nights giving way to mornings bright and clear.

Every ten days or so, Kyle and Emil left their helpers in charge and returned to the main house where they spent hours with Art and his maps of the range, reporting which streams and springs were running and which were dry, pointing out where the grass was good and where the herds were grazing.

"The Angus look good right now. I got 'em down on the old Halverson place where he had hayfields," Emil reported.

"Don't let 'em stay too long," Art said. "I don't want 'em eating on those weeds that come up in plowed ground. Kyle, any luck with that big red bull?"

"Not much. He didn't give me any trouble on the way out, but when I got him in with the cows and steers, he just went to grazin'."

"Maybe he's hung around steers so much he thinks he *is* one." Emil grinned.

"And where are you off to next?" Fontana asked.

They were walking in the twilight together along the road overlooking the river. The evening bugs were being a nuisance, but they just slapped them away and went on talking.

"Back to the south range, I guess, down by Willow Creek. Probably depends on that ol' red bull, whether I move the herd on over to Deer Lick or not. If he's doin' his job, I'll just leave them alone. Wouldn't mind a couple of weeks at Deer Lick, though. It's a park up in the mountains."

"You like working with cattle, don't you, Kyle?" She smiled at him. "I can hear it in your voice."

"Yeah, I really do. Oh, it gets boring sometimes. Sometimes too cold or too lonely, but it's good to sit a horse watchin' 'em. You see 'em gettin' fat, or havin' calves by their sides, and you feel like you've done a pretty good job."

They walked on, swatting at bugs and watching the dusk descend into early darkness.

"What about you," Kyle asked. "You happy? Doing the accounting and so forth for Art, I mean."

"Yes, I am. I suppose it's like you and the cattle. It can get boring at times, but when everything adds up and comes out right, it gives me a feeling of accomplishment. I feel needed."

"I suppose I'd be . . . nervous, I guess, about seein' all of Art's finances in front of me. Knowin' that much about his affairs, I mean."

"You get used to it, like being responsible for all those cattle he has such a big stake in. Do you ever think of getting a herd of your own?"

"Sure. What cowboy doesn't?"

"Will it ever happen?"

"Probably. Every so often I'll come across a real maverick calf or an unbranded stray, and Art lets his hands claim those as 'found'. And when I can, I'm goin' to buy some breed stock from him. He'll let me run mine with his, he said. I'll get a start, one of these days."

"And I'll keep the records for you!" Fontana laughed.

Kyle laughed even harder and took a tiny notebook from his vest pocket. It was only a half inch thick and the size of a gent's calling card. From another pocket he fished out a stubby pencil. He held these out to her.

"Here you go." He smiled. "Here's your bookkeepin' equipment. Everything I own and everything I owe is written down right here."

Fontana opened the little book randomly. In blunt pencil under **STOCK** she found such entries as: **j10 1mvk rt dbl notch, hi rng**.

"What's this?" she asked, pointing.

"Hmm? Let's see. That j means either June or July. Or January. The tenth. Found a maverick calf. I put my double notch mark on his right ear. Hi rng means I found him on the high range."

"No brand?"

"Never figured one out. Somewhere in there you'll see some pages covered with my ideas for a brand, but I never settled on one. I'm such a poor cowpoke that I don't even own a brand. If I was to 'endow thee with all my worldly goods', like they say at weddin's, you wouldn't get much!"

Fontana looked up into his face.

"I accept." She smiled.

And the twilight bugs found themselves in less danger, since the two humans held hands as they turned and strolled back toward the lighted windows of the Keystone.

They stopped from time to time, but it was not to swat at mosquitoes.

"Got word yesterday that Reverend Buchanan's stayin' down at the Two Bar," Art remarked as he and Kyle were riding toward the McCarthy place. It was in hill country on the northwest corner of the Keystone.

"Oh?"

"His circuit generally brings him here next," Art explained. "I figure he'll stay with us a couple of days."

"I suppose that's right," Kyle agreed. "I'll try t' get to his Sunday service then."

"Thought y' might want to talk t' him personal," Art said. "You know, there's a certain point nowadays when a man oughta talk with a preacher about things. Marriage and things."

Kyle laughed. Had Art brought him this far from the ranch to bring up the subject of marriage?

"That obvious, is it?" he asked.

"That obvious. Everybody but the ranch dogs can see you and Fontana have a thing goin' between you. Even the dogs are gettin' suspicious."

"We don't exactly hide it." Kyle grinned. "And I guess you're right . . . about fixin' up a time and place, and all. I'll have a talk with the reverend. So is that why we rode all the way out here?"

"Not really. I thought we'd take a good look at the old Everitt place . . . the McCarthy place . . . and I'd try a few ideas out on you. These bad days have hit everybody real hard. Like the Widow McCarthy. You remember her. We did all we could t' keep her and the boys goin', but finally she just had t' pull out, and so I gave her a good price on the homestead to help her. And I'm sort of stuck with it."

"So who's in it now?" Kyle asked, remembering the kind woman and the boy who offered him shelter the night he rode away.

"Nobody. That's the problem. It's a pretty good house, good pole barn, sheds. Old man Everitt, when he had the place, dug a good cellar under the kitchen."

"Make somebody a good farm, maybe?" Kyle said.

"I dunno. Not much water, when y' get right down to it. There's a small creek and a well. Widow McCarthy grew quite a bit of garden truck and managed to sell most of it, but there's no money in that kind of operation. No, I thought I'd make a breedin' station out of it. Put some of those Brahma bulls in there, or longhorn bulls. Might even bring in some heavy stud horses and try breedin' horses t' sell to farmers and freighters. If you want to make a go out of crossbreeding, you need a place where that's all you do. A place you can winter the stock and keep an eye on 'em."

They rode on. Kyle noticed the sharp incense of the sun-warmed pine trees as they crossed over a forested hill. They watched a grouse flap away from the trail pretending to have a broken wing. Kyle pointed skyward at a pair of eagles circling and sailing and crying to each other.

As they came in sight of the McCarthy place, Art got back to the topic.

"Another problem," he said, as if they had been talking all the time, "is these range bums we got now. Too many men outta work. Most of 'em seem OK, but Link, Will, Bob . . . a lot of us . . . have found signs they're livin' here at the McCarthy place whenever they pass through. Before you know it, they'll be breakin' up the cupboards and floorboards for firewood and using the livin' room for a stable. You know the kind."

"Yeah," Kyle agreed. "I know the kind. Me and Emil

buried some of 'em. I guess they see the Everitt place and figure it's abandoned."

"Well, it is abandoned. But now here's my idea. How about if you and Fontana came down here and ran this place? Keep a watch over this whole corner of the ranch. Start up something like a stud farm or try some crossbreeds, like I said."

"I'd need help. A couple of good hands, at least."

"I've been thinkin' of Emil. He's turned out to be a top hand with cattle, in my estimation. Y' could build a kind of bunkhouse, maybe on that little rise of ground out there, where that cottonwood is."

Kyle looked. There was, indeed, a smooth low rise of good green grass topped by a young cottonwood. The grass on it was lush, and the cottonwood leaves had a fresh, moist luster to them.

"Be a shame t' clutter up that hill by buildin' on it." Kyle smiled. "How about th' other side of that bigger corral there?"

"That looks good, too. Build it wherever y' want. Besides Emil, I'm thinkin' of givin' y' Cochran for a hand. Like I told you."

"The new kid," Kyle said flatly.

"Be good for him. I think y' could work the green off him if anybody at the Keystone could. Nobody takes the time with him, you know what I mean. He does somethin' wrong, we all cuss him or laugh at him, but we really oughta take time with him."

"Guess that'd work out," Kyle agreed. "Hell, I love a challenge. An' that boy's a challenge if I ever saw one."

They dismounted and let the horses nibble at the grass on the hill while they sat in the shade of the little cottonwood, chewing on Mary's beef sandwiches. The house, the pole barn, the trees over by the small creek . . . it all seemed natural to Kyle, just like the day when he saw the Keystone again. And so, on the way back to the ranch, he agreed.

"First, I'd need t' bring Fontana down here and see what she thinks."

"She's been here, y' know. Stayed with Missus McCarthy a while, not long after you . . . uh, left."

"Yeah. Well, we'd better let her look it over again, anyway. I'll get her to ride down here with me one of these days. And we'll have t' talk to Emil and the new kid, too."

"Cochran," Art said.

"Yeah, Cochran. Wonder if I'll ever get used t' callin' him anything but 'the new kid'." Kyle grinned.

"What are you lookin' for?" Kyle asked. He'd lost track of the number of times Fontana had twisted her head around.

"Emil, I suppose," she said, bringing her attention back to the road ahead. "I always have the feeling he's somewhere nearby."

"Not today," Kyle said, shifting the reins to one hand so he could use the other to pat her arm. "He went with Bob, lookin' for strays up on Big Bear Creek. Anyway, here we are."

The buggy rounded a little hill on the two-rut road, and there was the old Everitt place, or the McCarthy place. They went through the gate, and Kyle halted the team.

"We were thinkin', Art and me, that we'd build a bunkhouse and cook shack over there, past the corral, on that bit of flat ground. He thought maybe that little hill with the cottonwood on it, but I think it's too pretty t' spoil."

"Oh, I think so, too," Fontana said. "Why is it so green there, do you suppose?"

"I asked ol' Pat about that, seein' as how he's been in this country since Noah went aground, and he says there must be artesian water there just under the surface. We might drill a well there and see if the water doesn't come bubblin' up."

"Possibly," Fontana said. "But if you tapped into it, you might dry it up. I'm not sure it's a good idea."

Kyle scowled. *Just like her,* he thought, *to look for the worst possibility. On the other hand, she might be right.* "Maybe," he said. "But it's OK. There's a good well near the house. We'll get a windmill. Matter of fact, I think I know where there is one we could use. Nobody's used it in years. I'll get a team and bring it over here."

They left the team in the shade of a pole shed and walked around, looking at the buildings. Fontana already knew some of the place's drawbacks. Some of the corral posts were cottonwood, she said. The McCarthy boys put them in and were proud of them, but, of course, they would quickly rot in the ground. Mrs. McCarthy had planned to have them replaced with cedar, once she got the time.

Fontana pointed out a place where the roof was sagging.

"We can shore that up pretty quick," Kyle replied.

They went around to the front of the house where a roofed porch gave an evening view of the hills rolling toward the mountains, and Kyle imagined himself already sitting there in a rocker, relaxing, at the end of a day. He was still imagining it when he heard Fontana's cry of dismay from inside the house.

"Oh, no! Oh, how awful!"

He hurried inside and found her standing by the fireplace. A couple of smelly bedrolls lay next to it, along with a haphazard stack of firewood consisting of broken fence posts and boards. Bean cans and whisky bottles were thrown into a corner. The fire had been allowed to spill out onto the pine floor where it left a big scorched area.

Kyle scowled. "Art said that range bums used the place sometimes. They figure it's abandoned, I guess. But we can clean it up in no time. We'll get that floor fixed, scrub the soot off the fireplace. It'll look good as new."

Fontana kept finding other things that made the house look less than "good as new." A window frame in one bedroom was warped shut and would need fixing. The stove was caked with soot and grease and had several inches of ash under it. Outside again, she said she wished the outhouse door faced the other way, away from the house. The soil in the kitchen garden was hopeless, all clay; they would need to haul wagonloads of manure and plow it into the dirt.

She saw Kyle stomp his boot heel on the trap door to the cellar, testing to see how solid it was. That trap door was one of her biggest objections to the way the house was built.

"You can see," she said, "this whole porch is built over the storm cellar or root cellar or whatever it is. Mister Everitt must have thought it would cave in . . . look how thick those floor joists must be. It makes the porch floor higher than the kitchen floor. We'd trip over it every time we went through the door. And, besides, he made that trap door too heavy for one person to lift. Look."

She indicated the pulley lashed to a roof beam and the steel eye on the trap door itself. Evidently old man Everitt had a rope over the pulley to help him get the cellar door open. Kyle found a grip on the edge of the door. With great effort he opened it and leaned back against the wall. Steep wooden steps took him down into the gloom, and he had to duck under the thick logs Everitt had used as floor joists. The cellar walls were limestone rock and built like a bank vault.

There was nothing in the cellar except for a few rotting boards and a discarded demijohn jug. A moist, dank smell arose from the darkness.

"Best leave the door up and let it air out," he said.

Back outside, Kyle suggested a white picket fence. Fontana objected that a picket fence needs painting all the time. Kyle admired the tiny creek winding through willows, and Fontana muttered about mosquitoes and gnats. Finally, unable to come up with a single point about the place to which she didn't find some objection, Kyle unhooked the team and led them to the creek for water. He put them on long tethers so they could graze in the shade.

"I guess we can get to our picnic," he said hopefully, coming back to her.

"I hope you like what I brought." She smiled.

"Would y' mind if we walked to those trees across the hayfield? I'd kinda like to take a look over there and see if there's any we might use for corrals and such."

"I don't mind," Fontana told him. "A walk would be nice."

Kyle took the basket from her, and they walked east together with the midday sun beating down and a warm prairie wind in their faces.

"I kinda like how the wind blows your hair back that way," he said.

"Oh, really? I was just thinking that it makes my skin dry up like old paper."

The quarter mile stroll across what had once been a hayfield summed up just about everything that went wrong with the Wyoming cattle range that summer. They saw small thickets of cedar and wild plum where the branches were brittle and the boughs were more gray than green. They walked in knee-high grass that should have been waist-high, and it was dry and stiff. The ground was hard as rock. The wind should have carried a light scent of green hay, but it carried no message of life at all.

The ponderosas at the edge of the hayfield offered shade, and the dry grass made a cushion under the buggy robe. The field was fifteen or twenty acres of pale, dead stalks nodding in the breeze. Kyle stood looking it over while Fontana unpacked the lunch basket. *Still a heck of a beautiful day,* he thought. *And a beautiful place, when the rain comes back.* He picked up a fallen cone and rapped it against his open palm, making small winged seeds fall out. *A man could get a lot of these pines goin' out here,* he thought. *Grow his own firewood and lumber.*

And then he saw two riders coming up out of the hayfield toward them. When they got close, Kyle knew them for what they were—range bums. There was no mistaking the thin horses with droopy heads, the hats wrinkled and dusty from being used as pillows, the cracked leather of chaps and boots. But mostly what marked them as range bums was the dull and hopeless look in their faces.

Fontana quickly took up her plates of fried chicken and pie and put them back in the basket. Kyle loosened his Colt in its holster. The two men came as close as they cared to, one leaning forward with his arm on his saddle horn.

"Hi, folks," he said.

"Howdy," Kyle said.

"Havin' a picnic, looks like."

"Yup."

"That's fine. Don' got eny extra vittles in thet basket, I don' suppose."

"Nope."

"That's fine. Ya'll are welcome t' stay long as y' like."

"Oh?" Kyle said. "Your place, is it?"

"Shore. House is yonder. We just been out on th' range scoutin' the beef herd, y'know."

More like looking for strays to steal, Kyle thought. His eye traveled over their outfits, taking in the fact that their rifle scabbards were empty and so were their cartridge belts. Probably traded their rifles for food somewhere, and used up their ammunition on jack rabbits. One of them wore a holster that had been soaked and shrunk so often that it looked like it was stuck to the gun.

Kyle nonchalantly drew out his Colt and opened the loading gate and slid a cartridge into the empty chamber. He flicked an imaginary bit of dust off the front sight and casually dropped the gun back into its holster. Loosely.

"Guess I gotta disagree with you fellas," he said. "Truth is, this whole place, this whole range for miles in all directions belongs t' the Keystone Ranch."

It wasn't exactly the truth, since the old Everitt place stood on one corner of the Keystone on land the government still held open for homesteading. But these two waddies didn't know that.

"It's you what's got it wrong . . . ," the first one began to say.

"I ain't wrong," Kyle said. "Why don't you two ride back the way y' came, and keep ridin'. Don't leave the gates down."

Both riders stiffened and stared back at Kyle, their stubbled jaws set hard and their fists clenched. He might be a one-eyed son-of-a-bitch, but he packed a loaded Colt and was ready to defend his woman. This wasn't the time to start any fireworks.

"Got our outfits back at the house," the second man whined.

"I saw your outfits," Kyle said evenly. "If you mean

whisky bottles and a couple o' moth-eaten stinkin' bedrolls full of seam squirrels and fleas."

He drew the Colt and pointed southeast with it. "Kansas is that way," he said. "Why don't you two head for it. And don't look back till y' get there."

The two muttered and glared. Each looked at the other for a decision and got only a blank look in return. Finally they turned their horses and started plodding off back through the parched hayfield. The first one turned back just once.

"Y' ain't heard th' last of this, y' one-eyed bastard! Think y' own the damn' world! We'll show y'!"

Kyle laughed and aimed his pistol, thinking he might send a shot sailing just over the crumpled dirty hat, but on second thought it seemed a waste of ammunition. Instead, he watched until they jogged out of sight over the rise. He took off his gun belt and put the rig next to the blanket, then sat down.

"Let's see. You had some chicken there, I seem to remember?"

"You still want to stay here, after that?" she asked, amazed.

"Why not? Men like that, they won't be back. Just drift on, most likely find some kindly farmer who'll feed 'em."

"It's just that it ruins the whole idea of a picnic. I don't feel so. . . ."

". . . alone?" he asked.

"No, safe. No, that's not it. I don't feel like enjoying a picnic here, that's all. It's been spoiled." Her face was serious, full of concern, and he didn't like it.

"Fontana," he said in exasperation, "nothing's changed! Look! The sun's bright as can be, there's a nice wind comin' along and keepin' us cool, we've got shade here, and a big supper in the basket. Later on we could even go wade in the creek, back at the house, if you want to. Imagine how cold that water's gonna feel on your bare feet. Nice squishy mud between your toes. C'mon, let me see that chicken. What else y' got there?"

Kyle was lying full length, propped up on one elbow on the edge of the buggy robe. The wind cooled his back. Fontana fussed as it blew a dry pine needle into the pie tin, but Kyle just smiled and probed in the bowl of potato salad with his fork, looking for another big chunk of hard-boiled egg.

"Ever wonder who invented potato salad?" he said. "I don't suppose it was the Irish. I remember livin' on potatoes, and there didn't seem to be time to fuss around making salad with 'em. That'd be like a cow making a range grass salad."

"My recipe came from Germany."

Fontana went on tidying up, putting away the leftover chicken and rolls, wiping the plates, and taking out the small plates she had brought for pie.

"We'll need to find some good potato seed," she said seriously. "After you manure the garden and plow it, you'd better break some ground for a potato patch."

"Is that before or after I fix the floor and the windows and clean the stove and mend the fence?" He was smiling at her, but she was too busy fussing to notice.

Finally she looked up and began to answer. "Well, we can't possibly move until after the wedding, and that will be. . . ." She was looking over his shoulder, past him, with terror growing wide in her eyes.

Kyle rolled to his back and flipped himself to his feet, hauling the Colt from its holster, coming to a half crouch with the gun in his hand pointing in the direction Fontana was looking.

Bitter smoke full of flying ash hit his face. He saw a curtain of deep gray smoke cloaking the whole horizon. High curling waves of white smoke soared skyward just the other side of the rise, the other side of the hayfield.

The range had been fired. The prairie was in flames along a front a mile long, and the rising wind was bringing it straight at them.

Chapter Fourteen

BURIED ALIVE

"Wait! The basket!"

Fontana pulled her hand from Kyle's grip and turned back toward the fire to get the picnic basket and buggy robe. Kyle cursed, knowing there was no way in hell to outrun the flames. Their one chance—their only chance—was to make it to the stream on the other side of the house.

"Drop it!" he yelled. "Those don't matter! Drop them!"

But she ignored him. Or didn't hear him against the rising roar. She had picked up the basket and robe and was running back toward him as fast as she could. But her full skirts were a heavy weight against her legs, and she was lugging a cumbersome basket in one hand, the buggy robe dragging from the other. Kyle hurried to her and tossed his Colt aside so he could take the basket with one hand and grab her hand with the other.

"Now run!" he yelled over the roar. "Head for the house! Just run!"

Behind them the wind torched the whole hayfield in an instant, and the blood-red flame whipping through the dry stalks put up a thick blanket of white smoke. Above the roar and moan they heard a crackling sound; the grass around the field had caught. The smoke reached out ahead of the heat and overtook them, burning in their eyes and filling their nostrils with acrid stench. Kyle dropped the basket and kept pulling Fontana by the hand. She stumbled, went to one knee, screamed, rose again to be tugged along.

He looked back and saw the fire streaming up the tall trunks of the ponderosas where minutes earlier they had been sitting. A wall of dark red flame ran along the tall dry range grass, the smoke less dense and less white than the burning hayfield. At the edge of the grove behind the ponderosas it seemed to hunker down, coil itself, and leap into the lower branches of the trees. For a moment the trees resisted. But flames circled around the trunks and shot upward, heating the air rising into the branches where dry fuel waited. Kyle looked ahead again, squinting through the smoke to find the house and the creek. Behind he heard the double *WHUMPH!* as the crowns of the ponderosas exploded into torches.

Kyle's first thought was to get to the horses, but they would have bolted at the first smell of smoke. By now they were far away. At least they would make their way back to the Keystone, eventually, and somebody there would figure out that he and Fontana were on foot somewhere.

Fontana tripped and fell again, crashing her knee into rock, and nearly dislocating her shoulder, because Kyle was pulling at her arm so fiercely. She rose, limping, stumbled on with him. His boot caught in her skirts, and she dropped again, this time going down full length. The wind was knocked out of her, and for a minute she had no will to recover and get to her feet. Kyle turned back again.

"Get up! It's right on us!" he yelled over the noise of the fire. He put an arm around her waist and felt her slender body heaving and gasping for air in the smoke-thick surroundings. His own lungs and throat felt useless, full of air too hot to breathe. He lifted Fontana half off the ground with his one arm and hurried on, feeling the heat coming up off the ground and rising against his back, a heat so thick and intense it seemed to push him forward.

"Never make the creek," he gasped.

She cried out, her cry only a choked, dry sound against his shoulder.

They came to the horse trough in the yard. Kyle yelled at her to keep running while he stopped to plunge the buggy robe into the water.

"Too late for the creek," he said, sweeping the robe over Fontana's head just as he felt the heat crisping his own hair. The fire was so close upon them he could hear the individual crackle and pop of each sagebrush clump going up in flames as they ran past, each bunch of grass catching fire with a sound like someone striking a whole brick of lucifer matches at one time. Flame licked out toward his hair, his back. He imagined his vest and shirt being scorched as if with an iron.

"Down the cellar," he croaked. "Only chance we got!"

He pulled her toward the porch, his strength wreaking excruciating pain in her wrenched shoulder. He practically threw her down the steps into the darkness, and with her head covered in the wet robe she missed the last steps and sprawled head first onto the cool earthen floor. Kyle looked down, considered dashing down there to help her up, looked up out of the cellar hole at the fire coming onto the dry porch, the open window frames, and doorframe already bursting into flame. The smoke of the burning range grass had been sharp, acrid, choking. Now they faced the smoke of burning wood. The wind that slammed into the house was made ten times more powerful by the intense heat behind it, and it stung his face and his eye with bits of char. Flying soot, flying ash, flying embers swirled everywhere, following the two people down into the dark cellar hole.

Kyle took a deep breath with what little air he could find, then stood at the top of the stairs fighting to close the heavy trap door. Yellow flames rose and raged all around him, singeing his eyebrows and hair. The angle of the heavy door, leaning back on the wall, was against him. Standing in the stairway, he couldn't budge it. Then a sudden and unexpected strength surged into his body as he leaped out of the hole to stand on the floor itself, flames licking around his boots. He grabbed the upper edge of the trap door and pulled it over on himself. His arms over his head took the full weight, and he used his body to cushion the door's descent in case it should splinter when it hit the rim of the stone wall.

It closed with a *thud* and knocked Kyle to the floor beside Fontana where he plunged his head beneath the wet buggy robe to breathe the damp, earth-smelling air at last.

The inferno consuming the log house overhead wanted all the air for itself. As the floors smoldered and the walls flamed, the blaze sucked up more and more air and filled the structure with smoke as thick as cotton wool. The smoke curled around on itself, lunged at the walls, looking for a way out. The outer sides of the walls were all in flame. Inside, the air became hotter and hotter and the smoke thicker and thicker. A rafter cracked. Smoke rose into the attic with torch-like heat. Shingles began to smolder. Rushing up along the outside of the roof, the fire-driven wind found a gap, an opening. It tore off a weak shingle and gave oxygen to the superheated air; with a muffled explosion a hole blew out through the roof, and the smoke was free. New air was sucked into the rooms. The walls flickered into flame, and the flame roared for more air.

There was air under the thick floor of the porch, down in the cellar hole. Busily tearing apart the house, the flames wanted it. The fire could not reach down into the hole where the two people lay together, could not touch them, but it wanted their air for its flames and so sucked it up around the edges of the trap door. The couple lay breathing deeply, but then they were breathing with less heaving of their chests against the floor, and then they seemed to breathe as calmly as if they were asleep. And finally they were asleep under the robe together, all breath nearly suspended.

The fire had reached the house on a strong prairie wind, an upslope wind made fierce by the incomprehensible heat. It was that same strong wind that saved them. There had been grass and sagebrush in the yard for the fire to feed on, but with the grass gone and the house a pile of grotesque black timbers slowly collapsing in clouds of smothering ash, the firestorm subsided and allowed breathable air to seep around the charred door and down into the cellar.

The fire went away from the house as if no longer interested. It made a pass at the cottonwood trees and willow groves by the creek but found it was no longer intense enough to ignite the green grass or the green trees. It slowed down and crawled up the long open hills on both sides of the road, laid waste to all the fence posts it could, then slid out into sage and sand country where it gradually came to a smoldering stop.

Back at what was left of the house, two people lay unconscious in the cellar. Above them, the smoking walls buckled one at a time. The kitchen wall went first, letting the log ceiling rafters slide down onto the trap door. For a time the remaining logs in the porch roof stayed up, looking like drunken semaphores or abandoned hay derricks leaning against what little standing wall remained, and then they, too, came crashing down. They fell across the trap door, smoldering and crackling with red patches of glowing char. Anyone approaching the ruin of the house would see only a jumble of beams and logs and no sign of a door beneath, or a root cellar. Or two human beings.

Through the evening they shivered under the damp robe and huddled together for warmth. They slept. Sometimes one of them would awaken and realize darkness had fallen and would go back to sleeping. It was a restless night, painful to the back and hips and shoulders, the air clogging the nostrils and parching the throat. The blackness was total and seemed endless, but at long last there came an almost imperceptible lifting of the gloom.

"Kyle? Where are you?"

"Over here," he answered. "Looking for a way out."

"Have you found anything?"

"Not yet. These walls are quarry stone, laid up dry. No mortar. Pretty solid, though."

"What about the door?"

"I was waiting for you to wake up. Why don't you come on over here to the corner where the wall can protect you in case the whole thing collapses, and I'll give it a try."

She moved in the gloom, stretching out both hands before her, feeling her way. They touched hands, and he drew her into his arms. They stood like that for a long time, her hands caressing his back, his sooty face pressed into her hair that smelled of smoke. They sighed together, their chests heaving up and down together.

"Oh, Kyle," she said.

"I know."

"The whole place is gone, isn't it?"

"I s'pose so."

"What will we do?"

"I'm not sure yet."

They went on standing together, holding to each other, both of them staring into the darkness and both unable to think what to say. At last Kyle very gently removed his arms from her waist and shoulders and very gently pushed her away from him. She stood with her back pressed to the stone wall.

"Watch out for falling beams, now," he said. "I'm goin' to try to open the trap."

Kyle's foot found a couple of pieces of timber on the steps and kicked them out of the way. Standing on the first step, he reached up and felt the warm logs of the trap door. On the second step he felt the planking, and it was warmer, but not burning. He went on up to the fourth step and put his back against the center beam of the trap door. But when he straightened his legs and heaved for all he was worth, it was like trying to lift the whole house. Nothing budged.

He felt around for a prop, a lever, anything to wedge into the frame, but found only char-weakened bits of timber. They wouldn't take the weight, but he brought them to the stairs anyway and leaned them where he could grab them in case the trap door decided to raise an inch. He positioned himself on the fourth step again and put everything he had into an effort to raise the door, but it did not move. The roof and maybe even the walls had caved in on top of it. Way too much weight for a man to lift.

He could also hear popping and crackling on the other side of the door. The fire was still smoldering up above.

"Darling?" Fontana said in the dark. "It won't move, will it?" She was at his elbow.

"No. The damn' thing is blocked."

"If we both tried?"

"We could, but I don't think it will help."

They both got under it and pushed and strained at the weight, but the door remained as immovable as a stone slab set over a tomb. Kyle sat down on the steps and listened to the little popping noises. Up above somewhere, wood was still crackling. He might somehow break through the planking, but would that bring a shower of burning char down on them? He had to think about it.

Fontana moved off into the dark, and he heard her skirts rustling as she moved around the cellar. She returned to him, and he felt something thrust against him.

"Would this be any help?" she said. "Probably not."

She had found a thick, round pole, probably a shovel handle. Kyle's fingers explored it. Yes. A shovel handle, broken off at the socket. Four feet long or more.

"We'll give it a try," he said.

He forced the end of the handle into the planking, but it would not go clear through. He probed the ends of the trap door with it, then tried to stick it in between the trap door and the edge of the hole. No luck.

Kyle tried to remember what the porch looked like from the outside. Was the top of the hole level with the ground, or was it built up above the ground? *Level*, he thought. *The floor joists were set on top of the stone wall.*

As he thought of the floor joists, he heard a sudden cracking sound followed by more rapid popping noises, as if a joist had broken open and the air had rushed in to revive the fire.

Fontana's voice came from a corner.

"I found something else," she said, "but it's no use to us."

"Stay put," he said. "The floor might be getting' ready t' collapse on us. I'll come over there."

She had found the jug, a big demijohn made of heavy

213

clay, the kind used to store molasses or home brew. It had no cork, and whatever had been in it had long since evaporated.

"Wish it was full of water," Kyle said.

Fontana agreed. Nothing would be more blissful at this moment than water on her face and in her throat.

"I'm goin' to try something," Kyle said. "Stay here and watch yourself."

He felt his way along to the outside wall, the wall facing southeast, and used the shovel handle to probe up between the heavy log joists. The floor evidently had not burned—it was still solid. All the heat probably had gone straight up the walls and into the roof. Finally, near the corner where Fontana was crouching, the handle abruptly broke through. A rotten place in the sill log, maybe, or a pitch-filled knot the fire had burned out. Whatever it was, the handle went on through into open air, and, when he drew it back, a slender shaft of sunlight came streaming into the smoky cellar hole.

"That's better!" he said. "At least we can see what we're doin'!"

"No, no! Air will get in. It will set the floor on fire again, I know it will," she said.

"Maybe. But look at the sunbeam!"

"Oh, Kyle! Your face!"

He could not squeeze his head up under the sill far enough to see outside, but he could look along the narrow shaft of sun into the blue sky, the size of a dollar. He thought he had never seen sky look so wonderful.

"You're all burned," she said. "Oh, your poor face. Your hair is all singed."

Kyle came away from the little streak of sun and back into the inky, smoky dark of the cellar. He took out his

214

clasp knife and began probing between the hewn stones of
the wall. Finally, near the southwest corner, two rows of
blocks down from the sill, he found a loose one. He could
slide his knife blade along the top and both sides. He put
the knife away and felt for a fingerhold. He tugged and then
tugged again, wiggled the block back and forth, and, inch
by inch, it moved out of the wall and finally thudded to the
floor.

"What are you doing?" Fontana asked, peering toward
him through the smoky gloom.

"Starting a tunnel," he said. "Gonna dig us a way under
this mess. I'm thinkin' this is the strongest corner, least
likely to collapse on us. Give it a good breeze, that floor
might catch fire again. But we'd be OK over here for a
while. Where's that jug?"

She was a dark shape against the tiny shaft of sunlight,
and she brought it to him. Kyle took the jug and felt the
shape and size of it.

"Good," he said.

The block above the one he'd taken out was wedged
solid and wouldn't move. But the one underneath the hole
came away easily, making an opening big enough for a man.
He wouldn't risk trying to take out any more blocks since it
might bring the whole wall down on them.

"Here goes," he said. He picked up the heavy jug and
began tapping it against the square block of stone from the
wall, rotating it and tapping all around it, around and
around until he figured it was weakened. Then he brought
it down hard and it broke open with a dull cracking noise
that startled Fontana.

"What was that?" she said. "Kyle!"

"Just broke the bottom off this jug, that's all. Gonna dig
us outta here with it."

He began gouging away at the dirt behind the wall, using the broken jug as a scoop and the shovel handle as a digging bar. The backfill behind the stone wall was firm and solid, but wouldn't be too hard to dig through.

Now the dark memory of the cañon came back to him once more. And the words of the fortune-teller came back as well: he would travel east and a woman would follow and he would die but not die.

He could not get the cañon out of his mind as he dug at the dark earth. All he could think of was how he had spent—two years?—burrowing himself into the earth. When he was in the cañon all he wanted was to get away from the open sky, from people. From himself. Now all he wanted was to keep moving toward the sunlight and the air.

Kyle stabbed and scraped at the earth. He dragged dirt out of the hole until he had tunneled through the backfill and into solid ground where the digging would be slower.

He crawled backward into the cellar again and sat against a wall to rest.

"How are you doing?" he asked Fontana.

"Fine," she answered in the gloom. "Only I wish I could help. I feel useless just sitting here. If the tunnel collapsed on you I think I'd go out of my mind."

Kyle could not see her face, but behind her he saw the spot of sunlight on the cellar floor, a bright circle the size of a cinch ring.

"Say," he said, "I know what you could do. It's a kind of game my mother used to play with me. I was no bigger'n a peanut, and we lived in a room in a big city. She took in ironin'. And t' keep me busy, she'd tell me to sit by a little spot of sun comin' in a window and tell her what was in it."

"I don't think I understand," Fontana said.

"Come here where the sun is. C'mon."

They sat on the floor together, the sunshine patch between them.

"Now," Kyle said, "while I'm diggin', you tell me everything you find in this spot. You'll see. Pretty soon you'll start seein' things you'd never see otherwise. Look, see? See that little white pebble here? No bigger'n a pinhead. See that? Heck, I can see it, and I only got one eye."

She looked and put out her slim, soot-blackened finger to touch the pebble.

"Right," he said. "Now what else?"

"That gray pebble."

"Size of your thumb, that one?"

"Yes."

"I'll tell y' something else I remember from my mother doin' that. When she finished a stack of ironin' and she opened the door t' go out and get more off the line, I'd look out that door and it was like a whole new world. Suddenly I'd see everything at once, all the little things in the yard."

"There's another white pebble. And a gray one."

Kyle went back through the smoky darkness to get on with his tunneling. "What else?" he called.

"Dirt," she replied.

"What's it look like?"

"Dirt," she said.

"What else? Look close, now. Tell me." His voice was far away and muffled in the tunnel. Fontana sat staring into the spot of sunlight.

"Bit of wood. Silver color. Size of a fingernail."

"Which fingernail?"

"Pinkie!" she shouted. "White pebble, gray pebble, fingernail sliver of wood."

"And?"

"Dirt. Oh! Grains of dirt. I see them in the sun. Grains

217

of dirt. Like brown sugar, no, salt. No, little pin heads!"

"Pick some up!" Kyle called to her.

"How much?"

"Twelve grains," Kyle said.

"Yes," she said after a minute. "I have twelve in my hand. Some are softer."

"How many?"

"Five. Five are soft . . . I crumbled them with my fingernail. The others are hard, like tiny stones. Three are black. The rest are brown."

"Tell me again," Kyle said. As the tunnel angled upward, he made better time than he could have hoped for, the dirt yielding more easily to the sharp edge of the clay jug. The tunnel was almost the length of his body now. "Tell me again!" he shouted.

"Gray pebble. White pebble." Fontana almost chanted the words, her eyes focused on the brilliant little spot of sun. "Twelve grains of dirt, one sliver of wood, a tiny piece of straw. Or grass. Yellowish stem. Here's part of a bug, I think."

"What part?"

"A leg part? Here's another little piece of straw. Here's a broken bead somebody dropped. Just half of one bead. Here's a funny grain of dirt . . . it's a little chip of glass. Here's an inch of thread. Here's a seed. Here's a . . . oh!"

"What is it?" Kyle said from the tunnel.

"I think it's a mouse dropping," she said. She was quiet so long that Kyle backed out of the tunnel to check on her. Fontana was sitting by the spot of sunlight, peering down at it with strange intensity, and she was rocking back and forth a little, softly repeating each item, adding new items that the moving spot of sun revealed.

"Pebble, dropping, bug leg, thread. Dirt, two kinds,

sliver of wood, silver. A broken bead, just one, a seed, chip of glass. Now there's a big stone, long as my finger, stamped into the dirt. It has streaks . . . rust, mustard, ash, shiny grains."

Kyle went back to his digging. He made another couple of feet before he backed out into the cellar to rest.

"Feeling all right?" he asked.

"Yes," she said. "It helps to have something to look at. You don't have any light at all in there, do you."

"It doesn't matter," he said. "I know where I'm going. I just keep diggin' away at it."

"This patch of light," she said, "did you ever stare into a fire until you started to see pictures in it? Or ever stand on a bridge and watch the current until you feel like the bridge is moving upstream?"

"Sure. Lots of times."

"It's something like that."

"Well, just wait until you get outside. You'll see more than you knew was there."

Kyle left her and went back to his digging, and within minutes he smelled fresh air coming in through the grass roots in the sod. Thrusting upward with the shovel handle he broke through, causing chunks of charred sod to collapse into the tunnel. He pawed and scraped it past him and kicked it down the tunnel behind him before returning to stick his head out into the clear fresh sunshine.

Kyle looked around. The house had been reduced to a few blackened timbers and a stone chimney sticking up out of the smoldering remains. It was no wonder he couldn't budge the trap door—roof beams and a whole wall had fallen across it, tons of scorched wood completely hiding the cellar.

But while everything in the direction of the house was

black, charred, wasted, and ruined, in the other direction was the most beautiful sight he thought he had ever seen. The small green hill where the young green cottonwood grew. The fire had burned all the dry grass around it but left the green grass untouched. The grass circle protected the cottonwood. Not a leaf seemed to be damaged. Everything else was black, a sea of char with blotches of white ash marking where sage or yucca had blazed away into powder. But unbelievably there it was, an island of green grass and shade of green leaves.

He and Fontana were alive and one tree was alive. And it would be enough.

Chapter Fifteen

UP FROM THE ASHES

Kyle squirmed back down the hole and into the cellar. Fontana turned at the sound and blinked at the light coming through the tunnel. She stood up. He put an arm around her shoulders and stood with her, looking down at the spot of sunshine.

"Did y' see everything y' could?" he asked.

"A seed, dead. Bit of straw. Broken bead. Twelve grains of dirt, all shapes, some soft. Mouse dropping. Chip of glass. Piece of a splinter. Soot, very soft. Bug's leg. Thread. Stone the size of my finger, streaks of rust, mustard, red, yellowish. Ashes. Shiny little grains like salt or sand. See?"

She held her open palm up to him. In it she had carefully arranged a few grains of sand and a bit of black soot, the chip of glass, and the tiny bit of thread as if they were treasures.

"Yeah. Time t' put them back, now. We're going out."

"Is the fire over?" she asked, dusting her hands against her ruined skirt. "Everything is burned up, isn't it. Well, I'm ready."

"C'mon," he said.

Kyle crawled out first and reached back in to help her. In a moment they were standing together beside the smoldering remains of the house. They squinted in the bright sun. Their clothes were black with dirt and soot. Her shirtwaist and his shirt and vest showed dozens of holes from flying sparks. Her hair was tangled and singed, and the tears running down her cheeks left white streaks in the coal-black smudges.

As Kyle had done, Fontana looked around at the smoldering remains of the house, at the blackened grass and burned buildings. But then she also saw the trees and grass along the creek that had escaped the fire. Even more miraculous, the little hill with the cottonwood tree was still green.

Kyle led the way toward the green rise of ground, and, when they stepped from the scorched earth onto the green grass and walked up the slope to the cottonwood, it felt cool and fresh. Even the air seemed to have less fire smell in it. He helped Fontana sit down, and after a moment she lay back, full length, on the grass and crossed her hands on her breast. Compared with sitting on dirt in a dark, smoke-filled cellar, the grass seemed like a bed of luxury and the open sky was pure bliss. Lying there like that, she looked like a fire-damaged effigy, a fallen statue, except that her eyes were open wide and staring up into the branches of the tree.

"Look at all the colors of green!" she said. "Shiny dark green, dusty pale green, olive-colored twigs! Look at the little knuckles along each branch! And the leaves! They all have teeth along the edges, don't they? And look how the teeth point to the tip of the leaf. Do you see the little buds? The leaves have veins like little rivers running into a big one."

Kyle reclined on one elbow, looking into her smudged face.

"Kyle," she exclaimed, tugging his scorched sleeve. "Lie down beside me so you can look up through the leaves. Look! See that patch of blue?" She pointed upward where the leaves and branches made patterns against the sky. "See, it's a lion head. Oh, look! Over there! It's a witch! See the pointy hat, all blue, and her crooked nose?"

Kyle looked. And he saw. But he rolled back to his side and propped himself up on his elbow again. He would rather look at her than make pictures out of cottonwood branches. She was smiling so beautifully he couldn't take his eyes off of her. And her eyes! They danced with wonder as she discovered imaginary figures in the leaf patterns and saw tiny details of branches and twigs. She plucked a leaf and put it to her nose to inhale the sharp scent. A high white puff of cloud passing over the tree thrilled her and made her eyes shine as if she had been given diamonds.

She pointed out a black fuzzy caterpillar crawling on a leaf hanging near them, and she laughed in a way that made Kyle think of Julia, Gwen's friend. Julia had that quick way of liking things. But the thought disappeared almost as quickly as it had come.

Fontana sat up and began loosening the laces of her boots.

"Did you bring the buggy robe?" she asked him.

"I can get it. You want it?"

"Yes," she said. "And see if you can find a bucket or something to carry water in, will you? But first help me pull these off."—and she held out one foot to him.

He left Fontana flexing her stockinged toes in the soft grass and returned to the ruin of the house to crawl down the tunnel for the buggy robe. It was pretty much dry, and, when he got it outside and shook it, most of the loose dirt and soot fell off.

In the smoldering rubble of the cow barn, Kyle found a milking bucket, warm and discolored from the fire. A good bucket, riveted together instead of soldered. Examining it for holes, he suddenly began to smile at a memory of long ago.

Will, was it, or Dick Elliot? . . . anyway, he could re-member back when a pair of cowboys tried to milk an old range cow. Gwen and Julia wanted some milk and those boys were, by God, gonna get some. What a rodeo that had turned into.

He took the robe and pail back to Fontana. She had stripped off her stockings and was leaning back on her arms and looking up into the tree.

"Thank you," she said, smiling. "Now leave the robe here, and you go down to the creek and wash yourself, Kyle Owen. You look a sight! When you are finished, bring a bucket of water for me."

He obeyed.

Out of sight behind willows, Kyle pulled off his boots, stripped to the skin, plunged into the stream, and sat down. The water was freezing, at first, even though it hardly came up to his waist, but it was the best water he figured he'd ever sat in. He lay down full length to wash the smoke and stink out of his hair. He reached for his shirt and undershirt and rinsed them and scrubbed them with sand.

When Kyle came up the hill, his damp shirt in one hand and bucket of water in the other, Fontana was wrapped in the robe and sitting with her back against the tree. Her clothes were in a pile next to her.

Her eyes swept over his pale chest, the dark leather eye patch slanting across his damp hair, his teeth gleaming in a straight row as he smiled, the breadth of his shoulders, the bulge and sinew in his muscles. His damp dungarees clung to his hips. He set down the bucket and stood in the sun-light stretching his arm to get rid of the cramp. Fontana watched his arm muscles flowing and swelling under the skin.

She said nothing. She only stood up and stepped out of

the shade and into the sun.

"I found a good place for a bath," he said. "Cold, but the water's pretty clear. If you'd like to come on down to the creek. . . ."

"No," she said. "I want to do it here. I want you to wash me. Here. In the sunshine."

She let the buggy robe fall away from her body and tossed it toward her pile of clothing. Kyle's mind tried to form words to say that she shouldn't be naked, that she was not only naked but was standing out in the open, in plain sight of anybody, but his mouth only dropped open and no words came from it.

As if reading his thoughts, she answered: "We can see a long ways in any direction. We can see anyone coming long before they see us. Now please pour your water over me. Slowly! It's cold!"

Time stopped. The sun stopped moving and blazed down on them. The breeze stopped so that wispy ropes of smoke from dozens of smoldering places went twisting straight up into the sky. Kyle stood beside Fontana, letting cold rivulets of water dribble over her while she rubbed it into her hair and over her body. He thought of the irrigation ditch high in the mountains and how clear and how pure it had been. He remembered living in the big house, at Crannog, and how he used to hear the sounds of Fontana in her bath over his head in the room on the next floor. He thought of the cañon and his rancid dank cave and the tunnels he had lived in and how he had never cared to wash himself.

He poured more water over her and listened to it splashing into the grass. He remembered how it was to drink alkali water and how sweet fresh water tasted afterward.

"I think I'm getting clean," Fontana said. "It feels wonderful!"

"Wish we had soap," Kyle said. She turned this way and that under the trickle of water from the bucket, and, whenever her face was turned away, he studied her. When she turned and caught him looking, she laughed and he blushed.

"Would you mind going for another bucket of water?" she said.

He went to the stream and returned to find her wearing the buggy robe and searching the sky.

"Kyle!" she said. "Listen!"

It was the singing of birds. A flight of small birds, gray with flashes of yellow in their wings, wheeled in unison and glided toward the tree and called to each other. They landed in the high branches and went on warbling joy to the sky. Two more birds arrived, larger ones with louder voices repeating three notes over and over. And coming from the cottonwoods and willows by the creek was the cooing sound of doves.

Fontana put her arm around Kyle's waist and leaned into his body, and the both of them stood there, wondering at the singing of the birds. He looked down at her face and with one finger wiped away drops of moisture from her cheeks. After a minute she put aside the robe and braced herself for the cold water.

Kyle obliged, looking at her body as he rinsed it.

"Lucky," he said.

"What?" she said.

"Me. I bet there ain't a man in a thousand gets t' see his wife this way. In the sun and out in the open, and all. You're a beautiful sight."

She put her head to his chest.

"So . . . ," he began.

"So?"

"Uh . . . well, like I told you, Art wants to start a breedin' ranch here. I mean this grass'll come back better than before. I've seen it happen. One or two weeks of rain, and it'll come back. And I'll get some help and build you a better house. Build a new barn and corrals and such. By this time next year we'll be ready t' breed some fine stock. All the place needs is rain. What do y' think?"

Fontana took his hands and drew back to arm's length, and Kyle was suddenly embarrassed by her nudity and looked over her shoulder instead. But she examined his naked chest and arms closely, measuring him with her eyes, memorizing the texture of his skin, longing to run her hands over the hardness of his muscles.

"The rain will return," she said simply, knowingly. "I think we could start with children," she said softly. "Don't you think we'd make a good breeding pair?"

His neck was the first thing to turn red, then the flush crawled up his cheeks and made them burn. But when he heard her light laughter and looked down at her again, there was nothing to do but pull her to him. Her breasts were cool on his chest and her arms were cool as they encircled his waist, but her lips were as warm as they were full.

Later that afternoon, Kyle was leaning back against the tree looking east, and Fontana was lying on the robe with half of it folded over her. Neither of them was doing anything, or looking at anything in particular, being in that lovely languorous foggy mood all lovers have known. Fontana lazily turned her head and looked southwest, past the burned buildings and down the road.

"Who's that?" she said suddenly, rising to her elbow.

Kyle looked. His first thought was to reach for his gun, until he remembered losing it. It wouldn't be needed, however. The faraway figure in the dark hat, jogging up the road so easily and deliberately, could only be one man.

"Reckon it's our guardian angel," he said, "come a mite late. It's Emil."

"Emil?"

"Yep, that's him. I s'pose our team went back to the Keystone, and he's come lookin' for us. I'll go down there."

Without bothering to put on his shirt, Kyle strode down the hill and crossed the burned grass, his boots raising puffs of ash with every step until he was on the two-track road. He walked quickly, meeting Emil at the two charred stumps of what used to be the homestead's gate. Emil pulled up and sat there, leaning one elbow on his saddle horn, looking at the half-naked cowboy with the eye patch. He was grinning.

"Somethin' funny?" Kyle said.

"You tell me. Y' all right?"

"Never better."

Emil looked at the smoldering remains of the house. "What'd she do, burn down the house 'cause didn't she like th' furniture?"

"Nothin' like that. I run off a couple of range bums we found squattin' on the place, and I figure they fired the grass off t' the south. Prairie fire. The flames came at us like a damn' freight train, an' we had t' hide in the cellar. Then the house collapsed on it, or at least that's what it felt like."

"Y' all right, then?"

"We're all right."

"Huh. Well, what d' you need me to do?" Emil asked. "Maybe I oughta get after them drifters."

"Let 'em be," Kyle said. "They're probably still runnin'."

"What, then?"

"Got any food on you?"

"Mary sent along some sliced beef an' bread," Emil said, indicating the tote sack hanging off his saddle. "Few apples in there, can or two of peaches."

"She knows you're partial to those peaches," Kyle said.

"Like 'em better'n almost anything."

"Yeah. Well, tell y' what," Kyle said. "You take those and whatever else you'll need for lunch and head on back to the Keystone. You might leave me that canteen, if y' can spare it. Then if you'd bring us a couple of horses . . . no. No, make that a buggy. Meanwhile, we'll start walkin' and probably meet y' halfway."

Emil shaded his eyes to look toward the hill where he could see the woman sitting by the tree.

"Walk?" He said it with the flat disbelief of a range-riding cowboy to whom walking was something reserved for four-footed beasts.

"Yeah, we'd like t' just walk. Take in the sights better that way."

"Maybe I'd better stay with you two," Emil said. "What with you bein' out of your head, and all. Art said he'd send a couple more men if I didn't get back by suppertime. And those drifters could still be around here somewhere."

Kyle looked back at the green hill and the unburned tree and Fontana.

"No, thanks," he said. "You go on back like I said. Truth is, we don't need you."

Emil understood. He smiled and pulled out a can of peaches to stick in his saddlebag, then handed the tote sack to Kyle, along with the canteen. "Take one of my guns," he said.

"Don't need that, either," Kyle said. "Can't think of a

thing I'd wanna shoot."

"Well, I might not get back before dark."

"Fine. We'll just stroll in the twilight. Bring a lantern for the buggy if you want."

"You sure y' don't want a gun?"

"Positive," Kyle said.

Hand-in-hand, they walked along the road like two lovers on a Sunday stroll. Not far from the gate they found themselves back in grass and sage, the fire having raged in the other direction. Fontana was the first to turn and look back at the shallow valley, the green hill, the line of willows and cottonwoods fringing the little creek.

"It's a lovely spot," she said.

"I'm goin' to bring out the Keystone drillin' outfit, and put a well there," Kyle said, pointing at the grassy knoll. "Gotta be artesian water, right by that flat rock. Wouldn't that be somethin', to have water pourin' out of the ground for us?"

"Yes," Fontana said. "We can have a cistern, deep and cold. But the overflow . . . we'll let the overflow just find its own way down to the creek. No ditch."

They walked on, and Fontana discovered a smooth red stone beside the road. She picked it up and showed it to him.

"Look how pretty this is," she said. "The red color is so even, so smooth. It looks almost man-made."

"That's called pipestone," he said. "On account of the Indians used it to make peace pipes out of. Y' find it around here once in a while."

"We could call our place Pipestone Ranch!" Fontana said.

"Maybe."

They walked on. After a time the road crossed the meandering creek. Kyle swept Fontana up in his arms and waded across the ford, both of them laughing. As he set her down on the other side, she plucked an enormous flat leaf, a cottonwood leaf.

"Look," she said, "look how all these veins are like little rivers running into the main one. And this edge with all the sharp teeth along it, like a mountain range. Especially at sunset. Oh, Kyle, do you remember how the mountain range looks from Crannog, at sunset? Like a saw blade set on edge against the light. And look how strong this leaf is. Thin, beautiful, strong."

Kyle smiled at the delight he heard in her voice. Here was life again.

"Then that's it," he said. "We'll call it Cottonwood Ranch, and we'll tell people the name comes from that one cottonwood that lived through the fire. But we won't tell anybody about . . . well, what else happened under that cottonwood."

"And that's where you'll dig the well. And you'll hang a swing in the branches for our children."

"Right. And you know what, I already got our ranch brand figured out."

Kyle picked up a stick and made a diagram in the damp sand, and Fontana knew what it was. She saw a meaning in it that touched her to the heart. But she did not know, nor would she ever know, all that it meant to Kyle Owen.

He had drawn two links of chain, intertwined.

RIDE WEST TO DAWN

James C. Work

Will Jenson was the first rider sent into the mountains to investigate problems the homesteaders and ranchers were having. Will, however, was confronted by the silent giant known as the Guardian, whose job it is to keep trespassers away from the hidden valley. Disarmed and on foot, Will finally made it back—physically and mentally disabled by his ordeal. Now one-eyed Kyle Owens is being sent on the same quest, forewarned against what Will was able to remember. He too will meet the Guardian. But he will also encounter the exotic Luned, who may protect him or prove to be his greatest enemy, better armed and more capable, in her way, than even the fearsome giant.

GUNS IN
THE DESERT
LAURAN PAINE

This volume collects two exciting Lauran Paine Westerns in one book! In *The Silent Outcast*, Caleb Doorn is scouting for the U.S. Army when a small wagon train passes on its way to California. The train's path will take its members through Blackfoot country and the wagon master has foolishly taken a Blackfoot girl hostage. . . . In the title tale, Johnny Wilton, the youngest member of the Wilton gang, is shot and killed while attempting to set fire to the town. The surviving members of the gang plan a simple revenge—attack the town and kill everyone in it!

BORDER TOWN
LAURAN PAINE

Nestled on the border of New Mexico since long before there was a New Mexico, the small town of San Ildefonso has survived a lot. Marauding Indians, bandoleros, soldiers in blue and raiders in rags have all come and gone. Yet the residents of San Ildefonso remain, poor but resilient.

But now renegades from south of the border are attempting to seize the town, in search of a rumored conquistador treasure. With few young men able to fight, the village women and even the priest take up arms. But will it be enough? Will the courageous townspeople survive to battle another day?

LAURAN PAINE

THE KILLER GUN

It is no ordinary gun. It is specially designed to help its owner kill a man. George Mars has customized a Colt revolver so it will fire when it is on half cock, saving the time it takes to pull back the hammer before firing. But then the gun is stolen from Mars's shop. Mars has engraved his name on it but, as the weapon passes from hand to hand, owner to owner, killer to killer, his identity becomes as much of a mystery as why possession of the gun skews the odds in any duel. And the legend of the killer gun grows with each newly slain man.

___4875-2 $4.50 US/$5.50 CAN

THE ADVENTURES OF
COMANCHE JOHN
DAN CUSHMAN

Comanche John is a notorious road agent. If he has a last name, no one knows it. Yet his legend precedes him in the form of frontier ballads sung by teamsters and stagecoach drivers. His life is filled with danger and conflict, and although his activities often place him on the wrong side of the law, more often than not he ends up defending the innocent and fighting for what's right. *The Adventures of Comanche John* brings the reader into the thrilling world of Montana mining camps, wagon trains on the Oregon Trail, and stagecoaches everywhere.

ED GORMAN

GUN TRUTH

Tom Prine figured that a stint as deputy in a backwash
town like Claybank would give him a nice rest. Until, in
the space of just a few days, arson, kidnapping and murder
turn Claybank into a dangerous place Prine no longer rec-
ognizes. Secrets are revealed and at their core is a single nag-
ging question—is anybody in town who they pretend to
be? The townspeople claim they want Prine to clear up the
mystery, but do they really? And are the people who swear
they are his friends in fact the people who are trying to kill
him? Prine doesn't have long to find the answers to these
questions before the killers move in and make him just one
more victim.

HELL'S
CAÑON

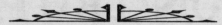

T. T. FLYNN

T. T. Flynn, author of such Western classics as *The Man From Laramie* and *Two Faces West*, is at his thrilling best in this collection of Western stories combining mystery, suspense, and action in artful combination. Whether they deal with Mississippi riverboats, wild mustangs, frontier prisons, or a man trying to escape his past, the stories in this volume all feature the sense of realism and emotional truth that have come to be associated with T. T. Flynn, a writer whose ability to depict the humanity of the West is unsurpassed.

T. T. FLYNN
THE DEVIL'S LODE

Since the Golden Age of Western fiction, the name T. T. Flynn has been a guarantee of excitement and adventure. His classic novels *The Man From Laramie* and *Two Faces West* were both made into equally classic movies. Now, for the first time in paperback, three of his best short novels offer abundant evidence of his glowing talents. Perhaps no better example of Flynn's abilities can be found than the title tale, in which Paso Brand is hired to work as a guard at a gold mine—only to be attacked by outlaws before he can even report for work. Outlaws and gunmen, ranchers and lawmen, the daring men and women of the West come alive again in the writing of T. T. Flynn!

MAR 8 2004